YOUNG
MONSTERS

*Upcoming anthologies
to be edited by Isaac Asimov,
Martin H. Greenberg and Charles G. Waugh:*

YOUNG ROBOTS AND ANDROIDS
YOUNG GHOSTS
YOUNG STAR TRAVELERS

Already published:

YOUNG MUTANTS
YOUNG EXTRATERRESTRIALS

YOUNG MONSTERS

EDITED BY

Isaac Asimov,
Martin H. Greenberg
and Charles G. Waugh

HARPER & ROW, PUBLISHERS

Young Monsters

Copyright © 1985 by Nightfall, Inc., Martin H. Greenberg, and Charles G. Waugh
All rights reserved. No part of this book may be used or reproduced in any manner whatsoever
without written permission except in the case of brief quotations embodied in critical articles
and reviews. Printed in the United States of America. For information address Harper &
Row Junior Books, 10 East 53rd Street, New York, N.Y. 10022. Published simultaneously
in Canada by Fitzhenry & Whiteside Limited, Toronto.

Designed by Joyce Hopkins

1 2 3 4 5 6 7 8 9 10

First Edition

Library of Congress Cataloging in Publication Data
  Main entry under title:
  Young monsters.

  Summary: A collection of stories by a variety of
authors about young people with one common character-
istic—they are all monsters.
    1. Horror tales. [1. Horror stories. 2. Monsters—
Fiction.   3. Short stories]   I. Asimov, Isaac,
1920–   . II. Greenberg, Martin Harry.   III. Waugh,
Charles.
PZ5.Y842 1985   [Fic]   84-48352
ISBN 0-06-020169-X
ISBN 0-06-020170-3 (lib. bdg.)

Acknowledgments

"Homecoming" by Ray Bradbury. Copyright © 1946, 1974 by Ray Bradbury. Reprinted by permission of Don Congdon Associates, Inc.

"Good-by, Miss Patterson" by Phyllis MacLennan. Copyright © 1972 by Phyllis MacLennan. From *The Magazine of Fantasy and Science Fiction.* Reprinted by permission of the author.

"Disturb Not My Slumbering Fair" by Chelsea Quinn Yarbro. Copyright © 1978 by Chelsea Quinn Yarbro. Reprinted by permission of the author.

"The Wheelbarrow Box" by Richard Parker. Copyright © 1953 by Richard Parker. Reprinted by permission of Curtis Brown Associates, Ltd.

"The Cabbage Patch" by Theodore R. Cogswell. Copyright © 1952 by Perspective; copyright © 1980 by Theodore R. Cogswell. Reprinted by permission of the author.

"The Thing Waiting Outside" by Barbara Williamson. Copyright © 1977 by Barbara Williamson. From *Ellery Queen's Mystery Magazine,* December, 1977. Reprinted by permission of the author.

"Red as Blood" by Tanith Lee. Copyright © 1979 by Mercury Press, Inc. From *The Magazine of Fantasy and Science Fiction.* Reprinted by permission of Don Congdon Associates, Inc.

"Fritzchen" by Charles Beaumont. Copyright © 1953, 1981 by Charles Beaumont. Reprinted by permission of Don Congdon Associates, Inc.

"The Young One" by Jerome Bixby. Copyright © 1953 by Ziff-Davis Publishing Co.; copyright © 1981 by Jerome Bixby. Reprinted by permission of Forrest J. Ackerman, 2495 Glendower Ave., Hollywood, California 90027.

"Optical Illusion" by Mark Reynolds. Copyright © 1953 by Standard Magazines, Inc.; copyright © 1981 by Mark Reynolds. Reprinted by permission of the Scott Meredith Literary Agency, Inc., 845 Third Avenue, New York, New York 10022.

"Idiot's Crusade" by Clifford D. Simak. Copyright © 1954 by Galaxy Publishing Corporation; copyright © 1982 by Clifford D. Simak. Reprinted by permission of Kirby McCauley, Ltd.

"One for the Road" by Stephen King. Copyright © 1977 by Maine Magazine Co., Inc. From *Nightshift* by Stephen King. Reprinted by permission of Doubleday & Company, Inc.

"Angelica" by Jane Yolen. Copyright © 1979 by Mercury Press, Inc. From *The Magazine of Fantasy and Science Fiction.* Reprinted by permission of Curtis Brown, Ltd.

Contents

The Power of Evil

by Isaac Asimov

Young people living in the United States or some other developed and industrial nation are used to inhabiting a universe ruled by the laws of science.

We know how to control the environment to what we think is our own benefit—to grow food more efficiently, to produce energy, and to control disaster. We know how to prevent many diseases from striking us, how to control or cure them if they do strike. We know how to lower the danger of lightning and how to make planes, cars, and machinery of all kinds quite safe to use.

Even when disaster does strike—when a plane crashes or a tornado hits or someone is murdered or gets an incurable disease—we know there are natural causes and, if we can, we try to find out exactly what those causes are and how to protect ourselves more efficiently against such unpleasant events.

How different things were in prescientific times—and, still are in many undeveloped regions today.

When science and modern thought did not exist, and

I

where they do not exist today, the universe is a strange and very frightening thing. There is no knowledge of the scientific laws that govern events. Things therefore take place without natural cause.

Floods come or droughts wither the landscape; storms batter at people or epidemics cut them down; lightning strikes or animals die of disease; somehow things go wrong.

Why? Why?

No one in nonscientific surroundings even dreams of seeking a natural cause. If something bad happens it must be because some intelligent being has caused it out of anger or spite. If the event is something no normal human being can bring about, then it must be some superhuman being who does it. One of the gods is angry because he or she hasn't been sacrificed to. A passing demon with a hatred for the human race inflicted them. An indifferent spirit is just amusing himself the way a child might when pulling wings off flies. Or perhaps the disaster is brought about by a just and kindly god who has been angered by sin, and who wishes to chastise the sinners.

But you don't know, you can't know, exactly what caused the event or how to prevent it. Does one beg the superhuman being for forgiveness, or threaten him, or make use of certain magical charms or rituals, or what?

And, of course, there is always the suspicion that some people are better informed on how to handle such gods and demons than others. Some people may have learned how to perform the rituals or how to say the charms in just the right way so as to prevent the supernaturally caused disasters or bring them to an end.

If these gifted ones are kindly, and are concerned with the good of the people, they are priests, seers, saints, wise men. But what if they are themselves selfish or evil and want to use their control over the supernatural to make themselves powerful or to punish anyone who offends them? Then they are wizards, witches, enchanters, necromancers.

Think how dangerous a universe would be if anyone you chanced to meet might be an enchanter, unknown to you. Some casual thing you say might annoy him and he might change you into a frog.

Then, too, once you become afraid of any stranger because he might be an enchanter, it doesn't take much to fear him (or her) because he might be a human being with horrifying abilities or habits—someone who looks like a human being, but who is so different in various ways that he might be considered a "monster."

What if he (or she) is not really alive, but is a ghost or spirit, an insubstantial remnant of a human being, who can take on the appearance of reality but who can disappear at will, and who means evil against you? Or what if he has the ability to change into a wolf (or some other animal) whenever he wants to; or what if he *must* undergo such a change even against his will at the time of the full moon. He is then a "werewolf." What if he eats dead bodies (he

3

is then a "ghoul") or drinks blood (he is then a "vampire"), and what if he lives forever as long as he can indulge these appetites, or what if he has superhuman strength or other abilities in addition.

In a world in which the idea of scientific law is absent, you don't ask how human cells can change into wolf cells, or how hair can suddenly grow when a man becomes a wolf, and what happens to it when the wolf changes back to a man. You don't think that a diet of corpses might result in food poisoning, or that an exclusive diet of blood might result in vitamin deficiency or in an iron oversupply.

Anything is possible, and as people tell these stories and pass them along, they get more and more horrible and horrifying.

In this anthology, we have collected over a dozen well-done tales of young monsters, those who are children or teenagers. Some are sympathetically, even humorously, told, and some are grisly.

But why should we be interested in such tales? Surely, we, with our familiarity with the scientific view of the universe, don't believe that such things as vampires and ghouls and werewolves can exist?

Yes, but we can pretend. In fact, that's what makes it fun. In the days when we thought monsters *really* existed, tales about them would have scared us so badly we would have nightmares, or be afraid to go out-of-doors. We would jump at every sound or shrink at every unexpected movement. Such stories would be no fun.

Nowadays, though, we can experience the odd world of nonscience, and even get tense or scared *while reading,* but then, when the story is over, dismiss it and return to our normal world where things happen out of natural cause and where we know what is impossible and what is not. We have the fun of *temporary* fear.

Then, too, in a way, to read monster stories is to move into a world so different from ours as to be a relief. Our own world has its terrors, too, though they are different from those of the nonscientific world.

We don't expect a stranger to be a dangerous enchanter—but he might be a dangerous mugger. We don't expect to meet a ghost or ghouls when we are passing a cemetery at night, but we might meet a car with a drunken driver at the wheel. We might not expect an angry god or demon to destroy the world in a fit of anger or malevolence, but human beings in charge of governments might destroy the world by nuclear warfare in a fit of fear or anger—or simple misunderstanding.

In a way, it is a relief to turn from the very real power of evil that surrounds us today to the totally different kind of evil that existed in the nonscientific world of ghosts and spirits and enchanters and monsters.

After all, we know that monsters *don't* exist—and that criminals and war *do* exist.

Homecoming

by Ray Bradbury

Exactly who is a "monster" often depends entirely on your point of view.

"Here they come," said Cecy, lying there flat in her bed. "Where are they?" cried Timothy from the doorway. "Some of them are over Europe, some over Asia, some of them over the Island, some over South America!" said Cecy, her eyes closed, the lashes long, brown, and quivering.

Timothy came forward upon the bare plankings of the upstairs room. "Who are they?"

"Uncle Einar and Uncle Fry, and there's Cousin William, and I see Frulda and Helgar and Aunt Morgiana and Cousin Vivian, and I see Uncle Johann! They're all coming fast!"

"Are they up in the sky?" cried Timothy, his little gray eyes flashing. Standing by the bed, he looked no more than his fourteen years. The wind blew outside, the house was dark and lit only by starlight.

"They're coming through the air and traveling along the ground, in many forms," said Cecy, in her sleeping. She did not move on the bed; she thought inward on herself and told what she saw. "I see a wolflike thing coming over a dark river—at the shallows—just above a waterfall, the starlight shining up his pelt. I see a brown oak leaf blowing far up in the sky. I see a small bat flying. I see many other things, running through the forest trees and slipping through the highest branches, and they're *all* coming this way!"

"Will they be here by tomorrow night?" Timothy clutched the bedclothes. The spider on his lapel swung like a black pendulum, excitedly dancing. He leaned over his sister. "Will they all be here in time for the Homecoming?"

"Yes, yes, Timothy, yes," sighed Cecy. She stiffened. "Ask no more of me. Go away now. Let me travel in the places I like best."

"Thanks, Cecy," he said. Out in the hall, he ran to his room. He hurriedly made his bed. He had just awakened a few minutes ago, at sunset, and as the first stars had risen, he had gone to let his excitement about the party run with Cecy. Now she slept so quietly there was not a sound. The spider hung on a silvery lasso about Timothy's slender neck as he washed his face. "Just think, Spid, tomorrow night is Allhallows' Eve!"

He lifted his face and looked into the mirror. His was the only mirror allowed in the house. It was his mother's concession to his illness. Oh, if only he were not so afflicted! He opened his mouth, surveyed the poor, inadequate teeth nature had given him. No more than so many corn kernels—

8

round, soft and pale in his jaws. Some of the high spirit died in him.

It was now totally dark, and he lit a candle to see by. He felt exhausted. This past week the whole family had lived in the fashion of the old country. Sleeping by day, rousing at sunset to move about. There were blue hollows under his eyes. "Spid, I'm no good," he said, quietly, to the little creature. "I can't even get used to sleeping days like the others."

He took up the candleholder. Oh, to have strong teeth, with incisors like steel spikes. Or strong hands, even, or a strong mind. Even to have the power to send one's mind out, free, as Cecy did. But, no, he was the imperfect one, the sick one. He was even—he shivered and drew the candle flame closer—afraid of the dark. His brothers snorted at him. Bion and Leonard and Sam. They laughed at him because he slept in a bed. With Cecy it was different; her bed was part of her comfort for the composure necessary to send her mind abroad to hunt. But Timothy, did he sleep in the wonderful polished boxes like the others? He did not! Mother let him have his own bed, his own room, his own mirror. No wonder the family skirted him like a holy man's crucifix. If only the wings would sprout from his shoulder blades. He bared his back, stared at it. He sighed again. No chance. Never.

Downstairs were exciting and mysterious sounds. The slithering sound of black crepe going up in all the halls

9

and on the ceilings and doors. The smell of burning black tapers crept up the banistered stairwell. Mother's voice, high and firm. Father's voice, echoing from the damp cellar. Bion walking from outside the old country house lugging vast two-gallon jugs.

"I've just got to go to the party, Spid," said Timothy. The spider whirled at the end of its silk, and Timothy felt alone. He would polish cases, fetch toadstools and spiders, hang crepe, but when the party started he'd be ignored. The less seen or said of the imperfect son the better.

All through the house below, Laura ran.

"The Homecoming!" she shouted gaily. "The Homecoming!" Her footsteps everywhere at once.

Timothy passed Cecy's room again, and she was sleeping quietly. Once a month she went belowstairs. Always she stayed in bed. Lovely Cecy. He felt like asking her, "Where are you now, Cecy? And *in* who? And what's happening? Are you beyond the hills? And what goes on there?" But he went on to Ellen's room instead.

Ellen sat at her desk, sorting out many kinds of blond, red and black hair and little scimitars of fingernail gathered from her manicurist job at the Mellin Village beauty parlor fifteen miles over. A sturdy mahogany case lay in one corner with her name on it.

"Go away," she said, not even looking at him. "I can't work with you gawking."

"Allhallows' Eve, Ellen—just think!" he said, trying to be friendly.

"Hunh!" She put some fingernail clippings in a small white sack, labeled them. "What can it mean to you? What do you know of it? It'll scare the hell out of you. Go back to bed."

His cheeks burned. "I'm needed to polish and work and help serve."

"If you don't go, you'll find a dozen raw oysters in your bed tomorrow," said Ellen, matter-of-factly. "Good-by, Timothy."

In his anger, rushing downstairs, he bumped into Laura.

"Watch where you're going!" she shrieked from clenched teeth.

She swept away. He ran to the open cellar door, smelled the channel of moist earthy air rising from below. "Father?"

"It's about time," Father shouted up the steps. "Hurry down, or they'll be here before we're ready!"

Timothy hesitated only long enough to hear the million other sounds in the house. Brothers came and went like trains in a station, talking and arguing. If you stood in one spot long enough, the entire household passed with their pale hands full of things. Leonard with his little black medical case; Samuel with his large, dusty ebon-bound book under his arm, bearing more black crepe; and Bion excursioning to the car outside and bringing in many more gallons of liquid.

Father stopped polishing to give Timothy a rag and a scowl. He thumped the huge mahogany box. "Come on, shine this up, so we can start on another. Sleep your life away."

While waxing the surface, Timothy looked inside.

"Uncle Einar's a big man, isn't he, Papa?"

"Unh."

"How big is he?"

"The size of the box'll tell you."

"I was only asking. Seven feet tall?"

"You talk a lot."

About nine o'clock Timothy went out into the October weather. For two hours in the now-warm, now-cold wind, he walked the meadows collecting toadstools and spiders. His heart began to beat with anticipation again. How many relatives had Mother said would come? Seventy? One hundred? He passed a farmhouse. "If only you knew what was happening at our house," he said to the glowing windows. He climbed a hill and looked at the town, miles away, settling into sleep, the town hall clock high and round, white in the distance. The town did not know, either. He brought home many jars of toadstools and spiders.

In the little chapel belowstairs a brief ceremony was celebrated. It was like all the other rituals over the years, with Father chanting the dark lines, Mother's beautiful white ivory hands moving in the reverse blessings, and all the children gathered except Cecy, who lay upstairs in bed. But Cecy was present. You saw her peering, now from Bion's eyes, now Samuel's, now Mother's, and you felt a movement and now she was in you, fleetingly, and gone.

Homecoming

Timothy prayed to the Dark One with a tightened stomach. "Please, please, help me grow up, help me be like my sisters and brothers. Don't let me be different. If only I could put the hair in the plastic images as Ellen does, or make people fall in love with me as Laura does with people, or read strange books as Sam does, or work in a respected job like Leonard and Bion do. Or even raise a family one day, as Mother and Father have done. . . ."

At midnight a storm hammered the house. Lightning struck outside in amazing, snow-white bolts. There was a sound of an approaching, probing, sucking tornado, funneling and nuzzling the moist night earth. Then the front door, blasted half off its hinges, hung stiff and discarded, and in trooped Grandmama and Grandpapa, all the way from the old country!

From then on people arrived each hour. There was a flutter at the side window, a rap on the front porch, a knock at the back. There were fey noises from the cellar; autumn wind piped down the chimney throat, chanting. Mother filled the large crystal punch bowl with a scarlet fluid poured from the jugs Bion had carried home. Father swept from room to room lighting more tapers. Laura and Ellen hammered up more wolfsbane. And Timothy stood amidst this wild excitement, no expression to his face, his hands trembling at his sides, gazing now here, now there. Banging of doors, laughter, the sound of liquid pouring, darkness, sound of wind, the webbed thunder of wings, the padding of feet, the welcoming bursts of talk at the entrances, the transparent rattlings of casements, the shadows passing, coming, going, wavering.

"Well, well, and *this* must be Timothy!"

"What?"

A chilly hand took his hand. A long, hairy face leaned down over him. "A good lad, a fine lad," said the stranger.

"Timothy," said his mother. "This is Uncle Jason."

"Hello, Uncle Jason."

"And over here—" Mother drifted Uncle Jason away. Uncle Jason peered back at Timothy over his caped shoulder, and winked.

Timothy stood alone.

From off a thousand miles in the candled darkness, he heard a high fluting voice; that was Ellen. "And my brothers, they *are* clever. Can you guess their occupations, Aunt Morgiana?"

"I have no idea."

"They operate the undertaking establishment in town."

"What!" A gasp.

"Yes!" Shrill laughter. "Isn't that priceless!"

Timothy stood very still.

A pause in the laughter. "They bring home sustenance for Mama, Papa and all of us," said Laura. "Except, of course, Timothy. . . ."

An uneasy silence. Uncle Jason's voice demanded. "Well? Come now. What about Timothy?"

"Oh, Laura, your tongue," said Mother.

Laura went on with it. Timothy shut his eyes. "Timothy doesn't . . . well . . . doesn't *like* blood. He's delicate."

"He'll learn," said Mother. "He'll learn," she said very firmly. "He's my son, and he'll learn. He's only fourteen."

"But I was raised on the stuff," said Uncle Jason, his voice passing from one room on into another. The wind played the trees outside like harps. A little rain spattered on the windows—"raised on the stuff," passing away into faintness.

Timothy bit his lips and opened his eyes.

"Well, it was all my fault." Mother was showing them into the kitchen now. "I tried forcing him. You can't force children, you only make them sick, and then they never get a taste for things. Look at Bion, now, he was thirteen before he . . ."

"I understand," murmured Uncle Jason. "Timothy will come around."

"I'm sure he will," said Mother, defiantly.

Candle flames quivered as shadows crossed and recrossed the dozen musty rooms. Timothy was cold. He smelled the hot tallow in his nostrils and instinctively he grabbed at a candle and walked with it around and about the house, pretending to straighten the crepe.

"Timothy," someone whispered behind a patterned wall, hissing and sizzling and sighing the words, *"Timothy is afraid of the dark."*

Leonard's voice. Hateful Leonard!

"I like the candle, that's all," said Timothy in a reproachful whisper.

More noise, more laughter, and thunder. Cascades of roaring laughter. Bangings and clickings and shouts and rustles of clothing. Clammy fog swept through the front door. Out of the fog, settling his wings, stalked a tall man.

"Uncle Einar!"

Timothy propelled himself on his thin legs straight through the fog, under the green webbing shadows. He threw himself across Einar's arms. Einar lifted him.

"You've wings, Timothy!" He tossed the boy light as thistles. "Wings, Timothy—fly!" Faces wheeled under. Darkness rotated. The house blew away. Timothy felt breezelike. He flapped his arms. Einar's fingers caught and threw him once more to the ceiling. The ceiling rushed down like a charred wall. "Fly, Timothy!" shouted Einar, loud and deep. "Fly with wings! Wings!"

He felt an exquisite ecstasy in his shoulder blades, as if roots grew, burst to explode and blossom into new, moist membrane. He babbled wild stuff; again Einar hurled him high.

The autumn wind broke in a tide on the house, rain crashed down, shaking the beams, causing chandeliers to tilt their enraged candle lights. And the one hundred relatives peered out from every black, enchanted room, circling inward, all shapes and sizes, to where Einar balanced the child like a baton in the roaring spaces.

16

"Enough!" shouted Einar, at last.

Timothy, deposited on the floor timbers, exaltedly, exhaustedly fell against Uncle Einar, sobbing happily. "Uncle, Uncle, Uncle!"

"Was it good, flying? Eh, Timothy?" said Uncle Einar, bending down, patting Timothy's head. "Good, good."

It was coming toward dawn. Most had arrived and were ready to bed down for the daylight, sleep motionlessly with no sound until the following sunset, when they would shout out of their mahogany boxes for the revelry.

Uncle Einar, followed by dozens of others, moved toward the cellar. Mother directed them downward to the crowded row on row of highly polished boxes. Einar, his wings like sea-green tarpaulins tented behind him, moved with a curious whistling through the passageway; where his wings touched they made a sound of drumheads gently beaten.

Upstairs, Timothy lay wearily thinking, trying to like the darkness. There was so much you could do in darkness that people couldn't criticize you for, because they never saw you. He *did* like the night, but it was a qualified liking; sometimes there was so much night he cried out in rebellion.

In the cellar, mahogany doors sealed downward, drawn in by pale hands. In corners, certain relatives circled three times to lie down, heads on paws, eyelids shut. The sun rose. There was a sleeping.

Sunset. The revel exploded like a bat nest struck full, shrieking out, fluttering, spreading. Box doors banked wide.

Steps rushed up from cellar damp. More late guests, kicking on front and back portals, were admitted.

It rained, and sodden visitors laid their capes, their water-pelleted hats, their sprinkled veils upon Timothy, who bore them to a closet. The rooms were crowd-packed. The laughter of one cousin shot from one room, angled off the wall of another, ricocheted, banked, and returned to Timothy's ears from a fourth room, accurate and cynical.

A mouse ran across the floor.

"I know you, Niece Leibersrouter!" exclaimed Father.

The mouse spiraled three women's feet and vanished into a corner. Moments later a beautiful woman rose up out of nothing and stood in the corner, smiling her white smile at them all.

Something huddled against the flooded pane of the kitchen window. It sighed and wept and tapped continually, pressed against the glass, but Timothy could make nothing of it; he saw nothing. In imagination he was outside staring in. The rain was on him, the wind at him, and the taper-dotted darkness inside was inviting. Waltzes were being danced; tall thin figures pirouetted to outlandish music. Stars of light flickered off lifted bottles; small clods of earth crumbled from casques, and a spider fell and went silently legging over the floor.

Timothy shivered. He was inside the house again. Mother was calling him to run here, run there, help, serve, out to the kitchen now, fetch this, fetch that, bring the plates, heap the food—on and on—the party happened around him but not to him. The dozens of towering people pressed in against him, elbowed him, ignored him.

Finally, he turned and slipped away up the stairs.

He called softly. "Cecy. Where are you now, Cecy?"

She waited a long while before answering. "In the Imperial Valley," she murmured faintly. "Beside the Salton Sea, near the mud pots and the steam and the quiet. I'm inside a farmer's wife. I'm sitting on a front porch. I can make her move if I want, or do anything or think anything. The sun's going down."

"What's it like, Cecy?"

"You can hear mud pots hissing," she said, slowly, as if speaking in a church. "Little gray heads of steam push up the mud like bald men rising in the thick syrup, head first, out in the broiling channels. The gray heads rip like rubber fabric, collapse with noises like wet lips moving. And feathery plumes of steam escape from the ripped tissue. And there is a smell of deep sulphurous burning and old time. The dinosaur has been abroiling here ten million years."

"Is he done yet, Cecy?"

"Yes, he's done. Quite done." Cecy's calm sleeper's lips turned up. The languid words fell slowly from her shaping mouth. "Inside this woman's skull I am, looking out, watching the sea that does not move and is so quiet it makes you afraid. I sit on the porch and wait for my husband to come home. Occasionally, a fish leaps, falls back, starlight edging it. The valley, the sea, the few cars, the wooden porch, my rocking chair, myself, the silence."

"What now, Cecy?"

"I'm getting up from my rocking chair," she said.

"Yes?"

"I'm walking off the porch, toward the mud pots. Planes fly over, like primordial birds. Then it is quiet, so quiet."

"How long will you stay inside her, Cecy?"

"Until I've listened and looked and felt enough: until I've changed her life some way. I'm walking off the porch and along the wooden boards. My feet knock on the planks, tiredly, slowly."

"And now?"

"Now the sulphur fumes are all around me. I stare at the bubbles as they break and smooth. A bird darts by my temple, shrieking. Suddenly I am in the bird and fly away! And as I fly, inside my new small glass-bead eyes I see a woman below me, on a boardwalk, take one two three steps forward into the mud pots. I hear a sound as of a boulder plunged into molten depths. I keep flying, circle back. I see a white hand, like a spider, wriggle and disappear into the gray lava pool. The lava seals over. Now I'm flying home, swift, swift, swift!"

Something clapped hard against the window. Timothy started.

Cecy flicked her eyes wide, bright, full, happy, exhilarated.

"Now I'm *home!*" she said.

After a pause, Timothy ventured, "The Homecoming's on. And everybody's here."

"Then why are you upstairs?" She took his hand. "Well, ask me." She smiled slyly. "Ask me what you came to ask."

"I didn't come to ask anything," he said. "Well, almost nothing. Well, oh, Cecy!" It came from him in one long rapid flow. "I want to do something at the party to make them look at me, something to make me good as them, something to make me belong, but there's nothing I can do, and I feel funny and . . . well . . . I thought you might . . ."

"I might," she said, closing her eyes, smiling inwardly. "Stand up straight. Stand very still." He obeyed. "Now, shut your eyes and blank out your thoughts."

He stood very straight and thought of nothing, or at least thought of thinking nothing.

She sighed. "Shall we go downstairs now, Timothy?" Like a hand into a glove, Cecy was within him.

"Look everybody!" Timothy held the glass of warm red liquid. He held up the glass so that the whole house turned to watch him. Aunts, uncles, cousins, brothers, sisters!

He drank it straight down.

He jerked a hand at his sister Laura. He held her gaze, whispering to her in a subtle voice that kept her silent, frozen. He felt tall as the trees as he walked to her. The party now slowed. It waited on all sides of him, watching. From all the room doors the faces peered. They were not laughing. Mother's face was astonished. Father looked bewildered, but pleased and getting prouder every instant.

He nipped her, gently, over the neck vein. The candle

flames swayed drunkenly. The wind climbed around on the roof outside. The relatives stared from all the doors. He popped toadstools into his mouth, swallowed, then beat his arms against his flanks and circled. "Look, Uncle Einar! I can fly, at last!" Beat went his hands. Up and down pumped his feet. The faces flashed past him.

At the top of the stairs before knowing it, flapping. Timothy heard his mother cry, "Stop, Timothy!" far below. "Hey!" shouted Timothy, and leaped off the top of the well, thrashing.

Halfway down, the wings he thought he owned dissolved. He screamed. Uncle Einar caught him.

Timothy flailed whitely in the receiving arms. A voice burst out of his lips unbidden. "This is Cecy! This is Cecy!" it announced, shrilly. "Cecy! Come see me, all of you, upstairs, first room on the left!" followed by a long trill of high laughter. Timothy tried to cut it off with his tongue, his lips.

Everybody was laughing. Einar set him down. Running through the crowding blackness as the relatives flowed upstairs toward Cecy's room to congratulate her, Timothy banged the front door open. Mother called out behind him, anxiously.

"Cecy, I hate you, I hate you!"

By the sycamore tree, in deep shadow, Timothy spewed out his dinner, sobbed bitterly and threshed in a pile of autumn leaves. Then he lay still. From his blouse pocket, from the protection of the matchbox he used for his retreat,

the spider crawled forth. Spid walked along Timothy's arm.
Spid explored up his neck to his ear and climbed in the
ear to tickle it. Timothy shook his head. "Don't, Spid.
Don't."

The feathery touch of a tentative feeler probing his ear-
drum set Timothy shivering. "Don't, Spid!" He sobbed
somewhat less.

The spider traveled down his cheek, took a station under
the boy's nose, looked up into the nostrils as if to seek
the brain, and then clambered softly up over the rim of
the nose to sit, to squat there peering at Timothy with green
gem eyes until Timothy filled with ridiculous laughter. "Go
away, Spid!"

Timothy sat up, rustling the leaves. The land was very
bright with the moon. In the house he could hear the faint
ribaldry as Mirror, Mirror was played. Celebrants shouted,
dimly muffled, as they tried to identify those of themselves
whose reflections did not, had not ever appeared in a glass.

"Timothy." Uncle Einar's wings spread and twitched and
came in with a sound like kettledrums. Timothy felt himself
plucked up like a thimble and set upon Einar's shoulder.
"Don't feel badly, Nephew Timothy. Each to his own, each
in his own way. How much better things are for you. How
rich. The world's dead for us. We've seen so much of it,
believe me. Life's best to those who live the least of it.
It's worth more per ounce, Timothy, remember that."

The rest of the black morning, from midnight on, Uncle
Einar led him about the house, from room to room, weaving

and singing. A horde of late arrivals set the entire hilarity off afresh. Great-great-great-great and a thousand more great-greats-Grandmama was there, wrapped in Egyptian cerements. She said not a word, but lay straight as a burnt ironing board against the wall, her eye hollows cupping a distant, wise, silent glimmering. At the breakfast, at four in the morning, one-thousand-odd-greats-Grandmama was stiffly seated at the head of the longest table.

The numerous young cousins caroused at the crystal punch bowl. Their shiny olive-pit eyes, their conical, devilish faces and curly bronze hair hovered over the drinking table; their hard-soft, half-girl half-boy bodies wrestling against each other as they got unpleasantly, sullenly drunk. The wind got higher, the stars burned with fiery intensity, the noises redoubled, the dances quickened, the drinking became more positive. To Timothy there were thousands of things to hear and watch. The many darknesses roiled, bubbled, the many faces passed and repassed. . . .

"Listen!"

The party held its breath. Far away the town clock struck its chimes, saying six o'clock. The party was ending. As if at a cue, in time to the rhythm of the clock striking, their one hundred voices began to sing songs that were four hundred years old, songs Timothy could not know. They twined their arms around one another, circling slowly, and sang, and somewhere in the cold distance of morning the town clock finished out its chimes and quieted.

24

Good-bys were said, there was a great rustling. Mother and Father and the brothers and sisters lined up at the door to shake hands and kiss each departing relative in turn. The sky beyond the open door colored and shone in the east. A cold wind entered.

The shouting and the laughing, bit by bit, faded and went away. Dawn grew more apparent. Everybody was embracing and crying and thinking how the world was becoming less a place for them. There had been a time when they had met every year, but now decades passed with no reconciliation. "Don't forget, we meet in Salem in 1970!" someone cried.

Salem. Timothy's numbed mind turned the word over. Salem, 1970. And there would be Uncle Fry and Grandmama and Grandpapa and a thousand-times-great-Grandmama in her withered cerements. And Mother and Father and Ellen and Laura and Cecy and Leonard and Bion and Sam and all the rest. But would he be there? Would he be alive that long? Could he be certain of living until then?

With one last withering wind blast, away they all went, so many scarves, so many fluttery mammals, so many sere leaves, so many wolves loping, so many whinings and clustering noises, so many midnights and ideas and insanities.

Mother shut the door. Laura picked up a broom.

"No," said Mother, "we'll clean up tonight. We need sleep first."

Father walked down into the cellar, followed by Laura

and Bion and Sam. Ellen walked upstairs, as did Leonard.

Timothy walked across the crepe-littered hall. His head was down, and in passing a party mirror he saw himself, the pale mortality of his face. He was cold and trembling.

"Timothy," said Mother.

He stopped at the stairwell. She came to him, laid a hand on his face. "Son," she said. "We love you. Remember that. We all love you. No matter how different you are, no matter if you leave us one day," she said. She kissed his cheek. "And if and when you die, your bones will lie undisturbed, we'll see to that. You'll lie at ease forever, and I'll come see you every Allhallows' Eve and tuck you in the more secure."

The house was silent. Far away the wind went over a hill with its last cargo of small dark bats echoing, chittering.

He walked up the steps, one by one, crying to himself all the way.

Good-by, Miss Patterson

by Phyllis MacLennan

Miss Patterson was a martinet who finally let a student drive her bats.

Miss Agnes Patterson's fifth-grade class sat rigid under the Gorgon eye of their teacher, waiting to be programmed into the next item on their tightly organized schedule. Motionless, backs straight, hands neatly folded on their desks, faces careful masks of respectful submission, they seemed unaware that it was the last day before Easter vacation, with school almost out and spring waiting for them beyond the open windows. The trees now lightly smudged with pink, the call of carefree birds, the rich warm smell of moist earth and new growing things seemed to hold no charm for them. Not one so much as glanced outside. Apart from discipline, there was something on the windowsill that they could not bear to look at: an empty hamster cage.

The cage awaited no new occupant. It was simply there, to remind them of their failure in their nature study project—a frippery of modern education that Miss Patterson had never quite approved of. The committee appointed to care for the little beast had forgotten to take it home with them over the Christmas vacation, and their teacher, seeing in this oversight a heaven-sent opportunity for a stern lesson on Responsibility, had left the animal to the fate its thoughtless guardians had abandoned it to. When they came back after their holiday, they found it dead, lying on its back, eyes closed, mouth open, stiff and cold. Miss Patterson's vivid description of the torments the hamster must have suffered as it starved and thirsted to death had left most of the children in hysterical tears. One thing was sure: none of them would turn his or her eyes in the direction of that reproaching cage, no matter what marvelous events might transpire beyond the window. They sat, subdued, fully under control. When their teacher cracked the whip, they would jump.

All except Corinna.

Defiant little witch Corinna! She sat in the corner like a cat wandered in on a whim, watching what went on with a cat's inscrutable smoldering stare, or turning her attention inward to mysterious thoughts of her own. She had a reputation as a troublemaker. She had been transferred from room to room all year as teacher after teacher refused to cope with her. Her parents had been called, but they refused to discuss the problem like good parents. They said that their daughter went to school because the law required it, and let the law make her behave, if it could. It was no concern of theirs.

She had been in Miss Patterson's class for little more than a week, and though she had as yet done nothing overt, in her mere presence the group was beginning to disintegrate. The children were restless, uneasy, like sheep who scent the wolf. Her contempt for the activities in which they spent their days was obvious. She refused to answer questions when called on, did no homework, turned in blank papers; and with her example before them, the others were beginning, ever so slightly, to get out of hand.

Miss Patterson was not disturbed. She had been dealing with troublemakers for twenty years, and she knew how to break them. Her methods were not subtle, but they were effective, and Corinna had put her most effective weapon to her hand by turning in an arithmetic test with nothing on it but her name. Miss Patterson returned the tests and addressed her pupils in a voice like honey on a razor's edge.

"Elephants have giant brains, and so all those who had perfect papers are elephants. Stand up, elephants, so we can see you. . . . My, we have a lot of elephants, haven't we? . . . Mice have little brains and don't pay attention, and so they make mistakes, but they can squeeze by. Stand up, mice! . . . Fleas are little tiny parasites with no brains at all. They're really stupid. We don't have any fleas in *our* class, do we? . . . Oh, we *do* have one! Corinna didn't get one single answer on this test! She couldn't answer *any* of the questions! Stand up, Corinna. You must be a very tiny flea indeed!"

She smiled triumphantly, and looked to see Corinna crushed.

"If I'm a flea, you're an old bat."

It was unthinkable that such impertinence could be. Stunned, helplessly conscious of her mouth gone slack, her burning face, Miss Patterson sat paralyzed. Transfixed by Corinna's eyes, fierce and yellow and soulless as a hawk's, she knew—how could she not have known before? How could she not have seen what she now saw so clearly?—this was no child like other children.

"You are a bat," Corinna repeated ominously, her witch's eyes grown huge and luminous. She glided forward, reached the desk and slid around it like a snake. Behind her, suddenly aware, bonded with her, strengthening her with their united wills, the children converged on their teacher. They gathered around her desk, all of them staring . . .

. . . Did they grow larger? Was it she who shrank? They loomed above her, glaring down with savage joy.

Agnes Patterson fluttered off her chair and scuttled away between their feet, screaming for help in a voice too shrill for human ears to hear. The children, shrieking their triumph, raced after her, chivvying her from corner to corner, striking at her as she dove past them. Help came at last, brought by the pandemonium in the room—Mr. Morgan from across the hall.

"What's going on here!"

"It's our bat!" Corinna shouted. "Our nature study bat! It got away!"

"Yes, yes!" the children chorused. "We're trying to catch it and put it back in the cage!"

"Where's Miss Patterson? She should have told me she was stepping out so I could cover her . . . never mind." He pulled off his jacket and in one deft swoop captured the hysterically chittering creature and stuffed it into the cage. He closed its door and glanced at his watch. "It's nearly time for dismissal. You kids sit quiet. I'll be keeping an eye on you from my room."

They took their places and sat until the bell rang. They said nothing aloud, but gleeful eyes met and giggles were muffled behind their hands as they gloated over the small animal huddled panting at the back of its prison. When it was time to leave, they gathered their things and left silently, in impeccable order, attracting no attention to themselves and their unsupervised classroom. Corinna waited until the others had gone. She came then and stood in front of the cage. The captive shrank still further back, but there was no move to harm her.

"Good-by, Miss Patterson," Corinna whispered. "Have a nice vacation."

She tiptoed out and closed the door behind her.

Disturb Not My Slumbering Fair

by Chelsea Quinn Yarbro

This most unusual story concerns the sin of gnawing pride.

It was already Thursday when Diedre left her grave. The rain had made the soil soft and the loam clung to her cerements like a distracted lover. It was so late, the night so sodden, that there was no one to see her as she left the manicured lawns and chaste marble stones behind her for the enticing litter of the city.

"Pardon me, miss." The night watchman was old, white-haired under his battered hat. He held the flashlight aimed at her face, seeing only a disheveled young woman with mud in her hair, a wild look about her eyes, a livid cast to her face like a bruise. He wondered if she had been attacked; there was so much of that happening these days. "You all right, miss?"

Diedre chuckled, but she had not done it for some time, and it came out badly. The watchman went pale and his mouth tightened. Whatever happened to her must have been very bad. "Don't you worry, miss. I'll call the cops. They'll catch the guy. You stay calm. He can't get you while I'm around."

"Cops?" she asked, managing the sounds better now. "It's not necessary."

"You look here, miss," said the night watchman, beginning to enjoy himself, to feel important once more. "You can't let him get away with it. You lean on me: I'll get you inside where it's warm. I'll take care of everything."

Diedre studied the old man, weighing up the risk. She was hungry and tired. The old man was alone. Making a mental shrug she sighed as she went to the old man, noting with amusement that he drew back as he got a whiff of her. She could almost see him recoil. "It was in the grave-yard," she said.

"Christ, miss." The night watchman was shocked.

"Yes," she went on, warming to her subject. "There was a new grave . . . the earth hadn't settled yet . . . and the smell . . ." *was delicious*, she thought.

He was very upset, chafing her hand as he led her into the little building at the factory entrance. "Never you mind," he muttered. "I'll take care of you. Fine thing, when a man can . . . can . . . and in a graveyard, too . . ."

"Yes," she agreed, her tongue showing pink between her teeth.

He opened the door for her, standing aside with old-fash-ioned gallantry until the last of her train had slithered through before coming into the room himself. "Now, you sit down here." He pointed to an ancient armchair that sagged on bowed legs. "I'm going to call the cops."

Diedre wasn't quite ready for that. "Oh," she said faintly, "will you wait a bit? You've been so kind . . . and understanding. But sometimes the police think . . ." She left the sentence hanging as she huddled into the chair.

The night watchman frowned. Obviously the poor girl didn't know what she looked like. There could be no doubt about her case. "You won't get trouble from them," he promised her.

She shivered picturesquely. "Perhaps you're right. But wait a while, please. Let me collect myself a little more."

The night watchman was touched. He could see that she was close to breaking down, that only her courage was keeping her from collapsing. "Sure, miss. I'll hold off a bit. You don't want to wait too long, though. The cops are funny about that." He reached over to give her a reassuring pat but drew away from her when he saw the look in her eyes. Poor soul was scared to death, he could tell.

"Uh, sir," Diedre said after a moment, realizing that she didn't know his name. "I was wondering . . . I don't want you to get into trouble, after you've been so kind, but . . ."

He looked at her eagerly. "But what, miss?"

She contrived to look confused. "I just realized . . . I seem to have lost my ring." She held up both hands to show him. "It was valuable. An heirloom. My mother . . ." Her averted eyes were full of mischief.

34

"Oh, dear," said the night watchman solicitously. "Do you think you lost it back there?" He looked worried.

She nodded slowly. "Back at the grave," she whispered.

"Well, miss, as soon as the cops get here, we'll tell them and they'll get it for you." He paused awkwardly. "Thing is, miss. It might not still be there. Could have been taken, you know." He wanted to be gentle with her, to reassure her.

"Taken?" She stared at him through widened eyes. "My ring? Why?" Slowly she allowed comprehension to show in her face. "Oh! You think that he . . . that when he . . . that he took it?"

The night watchman looked away, mumbling, "He could have, miss. That's a fact. A man who'd do a thing like this, he'd steal. That's certain."

Diedre leaped up, distraction showing in every line of her sinuous body. "Then I've got to check! Now!" She rushed to the door and pulled on the knob. "It can't be gone. Oh, you've got to help me find it!" Pulling the door wide she ran into the night and listened with satisfaction as the old man came after her.

"Miss! Miss! Don't go back there! What if he hasn't gone? Let me call the cops, miss!" His breath grew short as he stumbled after her.

"Oh, no. No. I've got to be sure. If it's gone, I don't know what I'll do." She let herself stumble so that the old man could catch up with her; if he fell too far behind, Diedre knew she would lose him. This way it was so easy to lead him where she wanted him. Ahead she saw the cemetery gates gleaming faintly in the wan light.

"You don't want to go back in there, miss," said the night watchman between jagged breaths. His face was slippery with cold sweat that Diedre saw with a secret, predatory smile. "Oh, I can't . . ." It was the right sound, the right moment. He automatically put out his arm. Pretending to lean against him, she felt for his heart and was delighted at the panic-stricken way it battered at his ribs.

"But I've got to find it. I've got to." She broke away from him once more and ran toward the grave she had so recently left. "Over here," she cried, and watched as he staggered toward her, trying to speak.

Then his legs gave way and he fell against the feet of a marble angel. His skull made a pulpy noise when it cracked.

With a shriek of delight Diedre was upon him, her eager teeth sinking into the flesh greedily, although the body was still unpleasantly warm. Blood oozed down her chin and after a while she wiped it away.

Toward the end of the night she made a halfhearted attempt to bury the litter from her meal. It was useless; she knew that the body would be discovered in a little while, and there would be speculation on the state of it: the gnawed bones and the torn flesh. As an afterthought, she broke one of the gnawed arms against a pristinely white vault, just to confuse the issue. Then she gathered up a thigh and left, walking back into the city, filled, satisfied.

By the time the last of the night watchman was discovered, Diedre was miles away, sleeping off her feast in the cool damp of a dockside warehouse. Her face, if anyone had seen it, was soft and faintly smiling, the cyanose pallor of the grave fading away to be replaced with a rosy blush. She didn't look like a ghoul at all.

That night, when she left the warehouse, she saw the first headlines:

NIGHT WATCHMAN FOUND DEAD IN GRAVEYARD

GRIZZLY SLAYING AT CEMETERY

Diedre giggled as she read the reports. Apparently there was some hot dispute in the police department about the teeth marks. There was also a plan to open the grave where the old man had been killed. This made Diedre frown. If the grave was opened, they would find it empty, and there would be more questions asked. She bit her lip as she thought. And when the solution came to her, she laughed almost merrily.

It was close to midnight when she spotted her quarry, a young woman about her own height and build. Diedre followed her away from the theater and into the many-tiered parking lot.

When the woman had opened the car door and was sliding into the seat, Diedre came up beside her. "Excuse me," she said, knowing that the old jacket and workman's trousers she had found in the warehouse made her look suspicious. "I saw you come up, and maybe you can help me?"

The woman looked at her, her nose wrinkling as she looked Diedre over. "What is the matter?" There was obvious condemnation in her words. Diedre had not made a good impression.

"It's my car," Diedre explained, pointing to a respectable Toyota. "I've been trying to get it open, but the key doesn't work. I've tried everything." She made a helpless gesture with her hands, then added a deprecating smile.

"I don't think I can help you," said the woman stiffly. She was seated now and had her hand on the door.

"Well, look," said Diedre quickly, holding the door open by force. "If you'd give me a ride down, maybe there's a mechanic still on duty. Or maybe I could phone the Auto Club . . ."

The woman in the car gave her another disapproving look, then sighed and opened the door opposite her. "All right. Get in."

"Gee, thank you," Diedre gushed and slipped around the car, slid into the seat, and closed the door. "This is really awfully good of you. You don't know how much I appreciate it."

The woman turned the key with an annoyed snap and the car surged forward. "That's quite all right." The tone was glacial.

She was even more upset when they reached the ground

level. The attendant who took her money told the woman that there was no mechanic on duty after ten and that it would take over an hour for the Auto Club to get there, and the locksmith would have to make a new key, and that would take time as well. Diedre couldn't have painted a more depressing picture of her plight if she tried.

"I guess I'll have to wait," she said wistfully, looking out at the attendant.

"Well," the man answered, "there's a problem. We close up at two, and there's no way you'll be out of here by then. Why don't you come back in the morning?"

This was better than Diedre had hoped. "Well, if that's all I can do . . ." She shrugged. "Where can I catch a bus around here?"

"The nearest is six blocks down. What part of town you going to, lady?" the attendant asked Diedre.

"Serra Heights," she said, choosing a neighborhood near the cemetery, middle-income, city-suburban. Altogether a safe address.

Reluctantly the woman driving the car said, "That's on my way. I'll drop you if you like." Each of the words came out of her like pulled teeth.

Diedre turned grateful eyes on her. "Oh, would you? Really? Oh, thanks. I don't mean to be a bother, but . . . well, you know." She added, as the inspiration struck her, "Jamie was so worried. This'll help. Really."

The woman's face softened a little. "I'll be glad to drive you." She turned to the attendant. "Perhaps you'll be good enough to leave a note for the mechanic so that there'll be no delay in the morning?" She was making up for her previously frosty behavior and gave Diedre a wide smile.

"Oh, thanks a lot for telling him that," Diedre said as the car sped out into the night. "I wouldn't have thought of it. I guess I'm more upset than I thought."

The conversation was occasional as they drove; Diedre keeping her mind on the imaginary Jamie, building the other woman a picture of two struggling young people, trying to establish themselves in the world. The woman listened, wearing a curious half-smile. "You know," she said as she swung off the freeway toward the Serra Valley district, "I've often thought things would be better with Grant and me if we'd had to work a little harder. It was too easy, always too easy."

"Oh," said Diedre at her most ingenuous, "did I say something wrong?"

"No." The woman sighed. "You didn't say anything wrong." She shook her head, as if shaking clouds away and glanced around. "Which way?"

"Umm. Left onto Harrison and then up Camino Alto." Camino Alto was the last street in the district, and it followed the boundary of the cemetery.

"Do you live on Camino Alto?" the woman asked.

"No. In Ponce de Leon Place. Up at the top of the hill." Behind that hill was open country, covered in brush. By the time the woman's body was found, the police would stop wondering about the missing one from Diedre's grave.

The car swung onto Harrison. "Doesn't it bother you, having that gruesome murder so close to home?"

Diedre smiled. "A little. You never know what might happen next."

They drove up the hill in silence, the woman glancing toward the thick shrubs that masked the cemetery. There was concern in her face and a lack of animation in her eyes. Diedre knew she would freeze when frightened.

"This is where I get out," she said at last, looking at the woman covertly. As the car came to a halt, Diedre reached over and grabbed the keys. "Thanks for the lift." She grinned.

"My keys . . ." the woman began.

Diedre shook her head. "Don't worry about them. I'll take care of them. Now, if you'll step out with me."

"Where are we going?" the woman quavered. "Not in there?"

"No," Diedre assured her. "Get out."

In the end she had to club the woman and drag her unconscious body from the car. It was awkward managing her limp form, but eventually she wrestled the woman from the car and into the brush. Branches tore at her and black-berry vines left claw marks on her arms and legs as she plunged farther down the hill. The woman moaned and then was silent.

It was almost an hour later when Diedre climbed up

the hill again, scratched, bruised, and happy. Tied to her belt by the hair, the woman's head banged on her legs with every step she took.

Taking the car, Diedre drove to the coast and down the old treacherous stretch of highway that twisted along the cliffs. Gunning the motor at the most dangerous curve, she rode the car down to its flaming destruction on the rocks where breakers hissed over it, steaming from the flames that licked upward as the gas tank exploded.

It was a nuisance, climbing up the cliff with a broken arm: the ulna had snapped, a greenstick fracture making the hand below it useless. Here and there Diedre's skin was scorched off, leaving black patches. But the job was done. The police would find the head in the wreck, along with one of the night watchman's leg bones, and would assume that the rest of the body had been washed out to sea: the headless woman back on the hillside would not be connected with this wreck, and she was clear.

But she was hungry. The night watchman was used up and she hadn't been able to use any part of the woman. Now Diedre knew she would have to be careful, for the police were checking cemeteries for vandals. And in her present condition the only place she wouldn't attract attention was the morgue.

The morgue!

Her broken arm was firmly splinted under her heavy sweater, her face carefully and unobviously made up as

Diedre walked into the cold tile office outside the room where the bodies lay. The burned patches on her face had taken on the look of old acne, and she used her lithe body with deliberate awkwardness.

"I'm Watson, the one who called?" she announced herself uncertainly to the colorless man at the desk.

He looked up at her and grunted. "Watson?"

Mentally she ground her teeth. What if this man had changed his mind; where would she go for food then? "Yes," she said, shuffling from one foot to the other. "I'm going to be a pathologist, and I thought . . . it's expensive, sir. Medical school is very expensive." Her eyes pleaded with him.

"I remember," he said measuredly. "Nothing like a little practical experience." He handed her a form. "I'll need your name and address and the usual information. Just fill this out and hand it in. I'll show you the place when you're done."

She took the form and started to work. The social security number stumped her, and then she decided to use her old one. By the time it could be checked, she'd be long gone.

"No phone?" he asked as she handed the form back.

"Well, I'm at school so much . . . and it's kind of a luxury . . ."

"You'll make up for it when you get into practice," he said flatly. He knew doctors well.

As he filed her card away, Diedre glared at his back, wishing she could indulge herself long enough to make a meal of him. It would be so good to sip the marrow from his bones, to nibble the butter-soft convolutions of his brain.

"Okay, Watson. Come with me. If you get sick, out you go." He opened the door to the cold room and pointed out the silent drawers that waited for their cargo. "That's where we keep 'em. If they aren't identified, the county takes 'em over. We do autopsies on some of 'em, if it's ordered. Some of these stiffs are pretty messed up, some of 'em are real neat. Depends on how they go. Poison, now," he said, warming to the topic, "poison can leave the outsides as neat as a pin and only part of the insides are ruined. Cars, well, cars make 'em pretty awful. Guns—that depends on what and where. Had a guy in here once, he'd put a shotgun in his mouth and fired both barrels. Well, I can tell you, he didn't look good." As he talked he strolled to one of the drawers and pulled it out. "Take this one," he went on.

Diedre ran her tongue over her lips and made a coughing noise. "What happened?"

"This one," said the man, "had a run-in with some gasoline. We had to get identification from his teeth, and even part of his jaw was wrecked. Explosions do that." He glanced at her to see how she was taking it.

"I'm fine," she assured him.

"Huh." He closed the drawer and went on to the next. "This one's drowned. In the water a long time." He wrinkled his nose. "Had to get the shrimps off him. Water really wrecks the tissues."

Five drawers later Diedre found what she had been looking for.

"This one," the man was saying, "well, it's murder, of course, and we haven't found all of him yet, but there's enough here to make some kind of identification, so he's our job."

"When did it happen?" Diedre asked.

"A week or so ago, I guess. Found him out in the Serra Heights cemetery. A big number in the papers about it."

Diedre stared at the bits of the night watchman. Something had shared her feast; she'd left more than this behind. It would be simple to take a bit more of him, here and there. No one would notice. But it paid to be careful. "Can I study this?" she said, doing her best to sound timorous.

"Why?" asked the man.

"To get used to it," she replied.

"If you help me out with ID, you can." He closed the night watchman away into his cold file cabinet. "In fact, you can do a workup on the one we just got in. Get blood type and all those things. This one hasn't got a head, so it's gonna be fun, running her kin to earth."

"Hasn't got a head?" Diedre echoed, remembering the woman left on the hillside. "What happened?"

"Found her out by the cemetery where they got the other. Probably connected. The grave she was found on was new and it was empty. Could be she's the missing one."

"Oh," said Diedre, to fill in the silence that followed before the man closed the drawer. She stared at the body, watching it critically. She hadn't done too bad a job with it.

"Any of this getting to you?" the man asked as he showed her the last of the corpses. Only about half of the shelves were filled, and Diedre wondered at this. "I'm okay." she said, then added, as if it had just occurred to her, "Why are there so many shelves?"

"Right now things are a little slow. But if we get a good fire or quake or a six-car pileup, we'll be filled up, all right." He gave her a shadowed, cynical smile. In the harsh light his skin had a dead-white cast to it, as if he had taken on the color of his charges.

Nodding, Diedre asked, "What do you want me to do first? Where do I work?"

The man showed her and she began.

It was hard getting food at first, but then she caught on and found that if she took a finger or two from a burn victim or some of the pulpy flesh from a water-logged drowner it was easy. Accident victims were best because, by the time the metal and fire were through with them, it was too hard to get all of a body together and a few unaccounted-for bits were never missed.

She was lipping just such an accident case one night when the door to her workroom shot open.

"Tisk, tisk, tisk, Watson," said the man she worked with.

Diedre froze, her mouth half-open and her face shocked.

The man strolled into the room. "You're an amateur, my girl. I've been keeping an eye on you. I know." He walked over to her and looked down. "First of all, don't eat where you work. It's too easy to get caught. Bring a couple of plastic bags with you and take the stuff home."

She decided to bluff. "I don't know what you're talking about."

He gave a harsh laugh. "Do you think you're the only ghoul in this morgue? I'm not interested in competition, and that's final. One of us has to go." He glared at her, fingering her scalpel.

It was quiet in the room for a moment, then Diedre put far more panic than she was feeling into her voice: "What are you going to do to me? What is going to happen?"

The man sniggered. "Oh, no. Not that way, Watson. You're going to have to wait until I've got everything ready. There's going to be another accident victim here, and there won't be any questions asked." He spun away from her and rushed to the door. "It won't be long—a day or two, perhaps. . . . Then it will be over and done with, Watson." He closed the door and in a moment she heard the lock click.

For some time she sat quietly, nibbling at the carrion in her hands. Her rosy face betrayed no fear, her slender fingers did not shake. And when she was through with her meal, she had a plan.

The telephone was easy to get to, and the number she wanted was on it. Quickly she dialed, then said in a breathless voice, "Police? This is Watson at the morgue. Something's wrong. The guy in charge here? He's trying to kill me." She waited while the officer on the other end expressed polite disbelief. "No. You don't understand. He's crazy. He thinks I'm a ghoul. He says he's going to beat me into a pulp and then hide me in drawer forty-seven until he can get rid of me. I'm scared. I'm so scared. He's locked me in. I can't get out. And he's coming back. . . ." She let her tone rise to a shriek and then hung up. So much for that.

When she unwrapped her broken arm, she saw that the ulna was still shattered and she twisted it to bring the shards out through the skin again. Next she banged her head into a cabinet, not hard enough to break the skull, but enough to bring a dark bruise to her temples. And finally she tore her clothes and dislocated her jaw before going into the file room and slipping herself into number forty-seven. It was all she could do to keep from smiling.

Somewhat later she heard the door open and the sound of voices reached her. The man she worked with was protesting to the police that there was nothing wrong here, and that his assistant seemed to be out for the night. The officer didn't believe him.

"But number forty-seven is empty," she heard the man protest as the voices came nearer.

"Be a sport and open it anyway," said the officer.

"I don't understand. This is all ridiculous." Amid his protests, he pulled the drawer back.

Diedre lay there, serene and ivory-chill.

The man stopped talking and slammed the door shut.

The officer opened it again. "Looks like you worked her over pretty good," he remarked, pulling the cloth away from her arm and touching the bruises on her face.

"But I didn't. . . ." Then he changed his voice. "Officer, you don't understand. She's a ghoul. She lives on the dead. That's why she was working here, so she could eat the dead. . . ."

"She said you were crazy," the officer said wearily. "Look at her, man," he went on in a choked tone. "That's a girl— a girl—not a ghoul. You've been working here too long, mister. Things get to a guy after a while." He turned to the men with him. "We'll need some pix of this. Get to work."

As the flashes glared, the officer asked for Diedre's work card, and when he saw it, "No relatives. Too bad. It'll have to be a county grave then."

But the man who ran the morgue cried out. "No! She's got to be buried in stone. In a vault with a lock on the door. Otherwise she'll get out. She'll get out and she'll be after people again. Don't you understand?" He rushed at the drawer Diedre lay in. "This isn't real. It doesn't matter if ghouls break bones or get burned. They're not like people! The only thing you can do is starve them. . . . You have to bury them in stone, locked in stone. . . ."

It was then that the police took the man away.

Diedre lay back and waited.

And this time, it was a full ten days before she left her grave.

49

The Wheelbarrow Boy

by *Richard Parker*

This is a story of a school where teachers learn to spell.

"Now see here, Thomis," I said. "I've just about had enough of you. If you haven't settled yourself down and started some work in two minutes' time I shall turn you into a wheelbarrow. I'm not warning you again."

Of course, Thomis was not the only one; the whole class had the fidgets; he just happened to be the one I picked on. It was a windy day, and wind always upsets kids and makes them harder to handle. Also, I happened to know that Thomis's father had won a bit of money on the Pools, so it was easy to understand the boy's being off balance. But it's fatal to start making allowances for bad behavior.

After about three minutes I called out, "Well, Thomis? How many sums have you done?"

"I'm just writing the date," said the boy sullenly.

"Right," I said. "You can't say I didn't warn you." And I changed him into a wheelbarrow there and then—a bright red metal wheelbarrow with a pneumatic tire.

The Wheelbarrow Boy

The class went suddenly quiet, the way they do when you take a strong line, and during the next half hour we got a lot of work done. When the bell for morning break went, I drove them all out so as to have the room to myself.

"All right, Thomis," I said. "You can change back now."

Nothing happened.

I thought at first he was sulking, but after a while I began to think that something had gone seriously wrong. I went round to the Headmaster's office.

"Look," I said, "I just changed Thomis into a wheelbarrow and I can't get him back."

"Oh," said the Head and stared at the scattering of paper on his desk.

"Are you in a violent hurry about it?"

"No," I said. "It's a bit worrying, though."

"Which is Thomis?"

"Scruffy little fellow—pasty-faced—always got a sniff and a mouthful of gum."

"Red hair?"

"No, that's Sanderson. Black, and like a bird's nest."

"Oh, yes. I've got him. Well, now." He looked at the clock. "Suppose you bring this Thomis chap along here in about half an hour?"

"All right," I said.

I was a bit thoughtful as I went upstairs to the Staff Room. Tongelow was brewing the tea, and as I looked at him I remembered that he had some sort of official position in the Union.

"How would it be if I paid my Union dues?" I said.

He put the teapot down gently. "What've you done?" he asked. "Pushed a kid out of a second-floor window?"

I pretended to be hurt. "I just thought it was about time I paid," I said. "It doesn't do to get too much in arrears."

In the end he took the money and gave me a receipt, and when I had tucked that away in my wallet I felt a lot better.

Back in my own room Thomis was still leaning up in his chair, red and awkward, a constant reproach to me. I could not start any serious work, so after about ten minutes, I set the class something to keep them busy and then lifted Thomis down and wheeled him round to the Head.

"Oh, good," he said. "So the gardening requisition has started to come in at last."

"No," I said, dumping the barrow down in the middle of his carpet. "This is Thomis. I told you . . ."

"Sorry," he said. "I'd clean forgotten. Leave him there and I'll get to work on him straightaway. I'll send him back to you when he's presentable."

I went back to my class and did a double period of composition, but no Thomis turned up. I thought the Old Man must have forgotten again, so when the bell went at twelve I took a peep into his room to jog his memory. He was on his knees on the carpet, jacket and tie off, with sweat pouring off his face. He got up weakly when he saw me.

"I've tried everything," he said, "and I can't budge him. Did you do anything unorthodox?"

"No," I said. "It was only a routine punishment."

"I think you'd better ring the Union," he said. "Ask for Legal Aid—Maxstein's the lawyer—and see where you stand."

"Do you mean we're stuck with this?" I said.

"You are," said the Head. "I should ring now, before they go to lunch."

I got through to the Union in about ten minutes, and luckily Maxstein was still there. He listened to my story, grunting now and then.

"You are a member, I suppose?"

"Oh yes," I said.

"Paid up?"

"Certainly."

"Good," he said. "Now let me see. I think I'd better ring you back in an hour or so. I've not had a case quite like this before, so I'll need to think about it."

"Can't you give me a rough idea of how I stand?" I said.

"We're right behind you, of course," said Maxstein. "Free legal aid and all the rest of it. But . . ."

"Oh, good," I said. "But what?"

"But I don't fancy your chances," he said and rang off.

The afternoon dragged on, but there was no phone call from Maxstein. The Head got fed up with Thomis and had him wheeled out into the passage. At break-time I phoned the Union again.

"Sorry I didn't ring you," said Maxstein when I got

through to him again. "I've been very busy."

"What am I to do?" I asked.

"The whole thing," said Maxstein, "turns on the attitude of the parents. If they decide to prosecute I'll have to come down and work out some line of defense with you."

"Meanwhile," I said, "Thomis is still a wheelbarrow."

"Quite. Now here's what I suggest. Take him home tonight—yourself. See his people and try to get some idea of their attitude. You never know; they might be grateful."

"Grateful?" I said.

"Well, there was that case in Glasgow—kid turned into a mincing machine—and the mother was as pleased as could be and refused to have him changed back. So go round and see, and let me know in the morning."

"All right," I said.

At four o'clock I waited behind and then, when the place was empty, wheeled Thomis out into the street.

I attracted quite a lot of attention on the way, from which I guessed the story must have preceded me. A lot of people I did not know nodded or said "Good evening," and three or four ran out of shops to stare.

At last I reached the place, and Mr. Thomis opened the door. The house seemed to be full of people and noise, so I gathered it was a party in celebration of the Pools.

He stared at me in a glazed sort of way for a moment and then made a violent effort to concentrate.

"It's Teddy's teacher," he bawled to those inside. "You're

just in time. Come in and have a spot of something."

"Well, actually," I said, "I've come about Teddy . . ."

"It can wait," said Mr. Thomis. "Come on in."

"No, but it's serious," I said. "You see, I turned Teddy into a wheelbarrow this morning, and now . . ."

"Come and have a drink first," he said urgently.

So I went in, and drank to the healths of Mr. and Mrs. Thomis. "How much did you win?" I asked politely.

"Eleven thousand quid," said Mr. Thomis. "What a lark, eh?"

"And now," I said firmly, "about Teddy."

"Oh, this wheelbarrow caper," said Mr. Thomis. "We'll soon see about that."

He dragged me outside into the yard and went up to the wheelbarrow. "Is this him?" he said.

I nodded.

"Now look here, Teddy," said Mr. Thomis fiercely. "Just you come to your senses this minute, or I'll bash the daylights out of you." And as he spoke he began to unbuckle a heavy belt that was playing second fiddle to his braces.

The wheelbarrow changed back into Teddy Thomis and nipped smartly down the garden and through a hole in the fence.

"There you are," said Mr. Thomis. "Trouble with you teachers is you're too soft with the kids. Here, come in and have another drink."

The Cabbage Patch

by Theodore R. Cogswell

"Ah, love! Where is thy sting?" It's an age-old question, but here is the answer.

Aunt Hester sent me to bed early that night. I lay quietly in the old four-poster, listening to the night sounds and the soft sleepy hisses as the narns who lived in the old fern tree underneath my window bedded themselves down in their holes. I was supposed to settle down too, but the tight, excited feeling inside my chest wouldn't go away. I pulled the soft down pillow over my head and tried to make everything black. I wanted to go to sleep right away so I could wake up in time to see the birth-fairy when she came down with my new sister.

Priscilla Winters said babies came from the cabbage patch but I knew better. She brought a cabbage to school one day to prove it, and that night when we were supposed to be asleep she opened it up and showed me a baby inside. It was squishy and white like all soon-babies are before they make the change, but I knew it wasn't a real baby because it didn't have any teeth. We made a birthing-box out of a jar and gave it some flies to eat but it wouldn't eat them, it just kept crawling around and waving its feelers as if it didn't like it there. When we woke up the next morning it had turned brown and was all dead.

The narns in the fern tree had stopped their whispering, but I still couldn't get to sleep. The little moon had chased the big one up over the horizon so far that its light was shining through the window right into my eyes. I got up and shut the blinds but even having the room dark again didn't help. I kept seeing pictures of the birth-fairy fluttering down like a beautiful butterfly, and then, after she'd put the babies safe in their birthing-box, flying off again with the year-father soaring after her on his fine new wings.

I wanted to see his wings but Mother wouldn't let me. For two months now she had kept him shut up in his room and she wouldn't even let me speak to him through the door. I wanted to say good-bye to him because, even if he was only a year-father, he'd been nice to me. I was never supposed to be with him unless Mother or Aunt Hester were around, but sometimes I'd slip into the kitchen when they were away and we'd talk about things. I liked being with him best when he was baking preska because he'd give me bits of the dough and let me make funny things out of them.

Once Aunt Hester caught me alone with him and her face got all hard and twisted and she was going to call the patrol and have him beaten, but Mother came in just then. She sent the year-father to his room and then took me into the parlor. I knew that she was getting ready for one of her heart-to-heart talks but there wasn't anything I could do about it, so I just sat there and listened. Mother's talks always got so wound in on themselves that when she was through I usually couldn't figure out what all the fuss had been about.

First she asked me if I'd felt anything funny when I was alone with the year-father. I asked her what she meant by "funny" and she sort of stuttered and her face got all red. Finally she asked me a funny question about my stinger and I said no. Then she started to tell me a story about the wasps and the meem but she didn't get very far with that either. She wanted to but she got all flustered and her tongue wouldn't work. Aunt Hester said nonsense, that I was still a little girl and next year would be soon enough. Mother said she wished she could be sure, then she made me promise that if ever my stinger felt funny when I was around a year-father, I'd run and tell her about it right away because if I didn't, something terrible might happen.

My pillow got all hot so I went and sat in my chair. The more I thought about the year-father, the more I wanted to go and see his new wings. Finally I went over to the door and listened. I could hear Mother and Aunt Hester talking in the front of the house so I tiptoed down the back stairs. When I got to the landing I stopped and felt around with my foot until I found the part of the next stair that was right against the railing. That's a bad stair because if you step in the middle of it without thinking, it gives a loud squeak that you can hear all over the house.

The year-father's room is right next to the kitchen. I gave a little scratch on the door so he would know who it was and not be frightened. I stood there in the dark waiting for him to open up but he didn't so I went inside and felt for him in his nest. He wasn't there.

First I thought maybe I should go back up and get in bed because Aunt Hester said that if she ever again caught me up at night when I was supposed to be sleeping, she'd give me a licking that I'd never forget. But then I started to think of what would happen to the year-father if he'd gone outside and the patrol caught him wandering around alone at night, and I decided that I'd better tell Mother right away, even if I did get a walloping afterward.

Then I thought that first I'd better look in the kitchen for him. It was dark in there too, so I shut the hall door and lit the lamp on the kitchen table. The stone floor was awfully cold on my feet and I began to wish that I'd remembered to put on my slippers before I came downstairs. Once my eyes got used to the light I looked all around, but the year-father wasn't there either. I was about to blow out the lamp and go and tell Mother when I heard a funny sound coming from the nursery.

I know it sounds funny to have a nursery in the kitchen, but since soon-babies have to be locked away in a dark place until it's time for them to make the change, Mother said we might as well use the old pantry instead of going to all the trouble of blacking out one of the rooms upstairs.

The big, thick door that Mother had put on was shut but she'd forgotten to take the key away so I went over and opened it a crack. I was real scared because at birthing time nobody is allowed to go in the nursery, not even Aunt Hester. Once the little ones are in the birthing-box, Mother locks the door and doesn't ever open it up again until after they've changed into real people like us.

At Priscilla's house they've got an honest-to-goodness nursery. There's a little window on the door that they uncover after the first month. It's awful dark inside but if you look real hard you can see the soon-babies crawling around inside. Priscilla let me look in once when her mother was downtown. They had big ugly mouths and teeth.

The sound came again so I opened the door. It was so dark inside that I couldn't see a thing so I went back and got the lamp. The noise seemed to be coming from the birthing-box so I went over and looked in. The year-father was hunched up in the bottom of it. He didn't have any wings.

He blinked up at me in the lantern light. He'd been crying and his face was all swollen. He motioned to me to go away but I couldn't. I'd never seen a father without his clothes on before and I kept staring and staring.

I knew that I should run and get Mother but somehow I couldn't move. Something terrible was happening to the year-father. His stomach was all swollen up and angry red, and every once in a while it would knot up and twist as if there were something inside that didn't like it there. When that would happen he'd roll his head back and bite down on his lower lip real hard. He seemed to want to yell but he'd choke it back until nothing came out but a little whimper.

There was a nasty half-healed place on his stomach that looked as if he'd fallen on a sharp stick and hurt himself real bad. He kept pushing his hands against it as if he was trying to hold back something that was inside trying to get out.

I heard Mother's voice calling from the kitchen and then Aunt Hester's voice saying something real sharp but I couldn't look up or answer. Blood was trickling out through the year-father's locked fingers. Suddenly he emptied out in a raw scream and fell back so limp that it looked as if all his bones were gone. His hands dropped away and from inside his stomach something tore at the half-healed place until it split and opened like a big mouth. Then I could see the something. I knew it for what it was and I felt sick and scared in a different sort of way. It inched its way out and wiggled around kind of lost-like, until it finally lost its balance and fell to the bottom of the box. It didn't move for a minute and I thought maybe it was dead, but then the feelers around its mouth began to reach out as if they were trying to find something. And then all of a sudden it started a fast wobbly crawl as if it knew just where it was going. I saw teeth as it found the year-father and nuzzled up to him. It was hungry.

Aunt Hester slammed and locked the pantry door. Then she made me a glass of hot milk and sent me up to bed. Mother came into my room a little later and stood by my bed, looking down at me to see if I was asleep. I pretended I was because I didn't want to talk to her, and she finally left. I wanted to cry but I couldn't because if I did she'd hear me and come back up again. I pulled the pillow down over my face real tight until I could hardly breathe and there were little red flashes of light in the back of my eyes and a humming, hive sound in my head. I knew what my stinger was for and I didn't want to think about it.

When I did get to sleep I didn't dream about the year-father, I dreamed about the wasps and the meem.

The Thing Waiting Outside

by Barbara Williamson

Here it is . . . good advice on how to really hound your parents.

A cold wind came down from the hills that night, and in their room under the peaked roof the children turned their faces toward the sound.

"It's only the wind," the father said.

"Just the wind," said the mother.

There were two beds in the room, a dresser painted white, and under the windows, a table with small bright chairs.

The walls of the room were light yellow, like the first spring sunlight. In their glow the dolls and fire engines, the pasteboard castle with its miniature knights, even the sad-faced Harlequin puppet shimmered with warmth. The plush animals became as soft as down, and the mane on the rocking horse was a crest of foam.

The children, a boy of eight and a girl of six, were already in their beds. The light glistened on their faces, their pale silken hair. They were beautiful children. Everyone said so, even strangers, and their parents always smiled and placed proud hands on their shining heads.

Now, in the yellow light, with the wind brushing the windows, the children listened to their father.

He sat on the side of the boy's bed and spoke quietly. The mother sat with the girl, her fingers now and then touching the sleeve of her daughter's nightgown. The faces of both parents were troubled.

The father said, "You do understand about the books? Why I had to take them away?"

The boy did not turn his eyes from his father's face, but he could feel the emptiness of the shelves across the room.

He said, "Will you ever put them back?"

His father laid a hand on the boy's shoulder. "Yes, of course," he said. "In time. I *want* you to read, to enjoy your books." He looked now at the girl and smiled. "I'm very proud of both of you. You read so well and learn so quickly."

The mother smiled too and gave the girl's hand a gentle squeeze.

The father said, "I think maybe this whole thing is my fault. I gave you too many books, encouraged you to read to the point of neglecting other things that are important. So for a while the only books I want you to read are your school books. You'll do other things—paint pictures, play games. I'll teach you chess, I think. You'll both like that."

"And we'll do things together," the mother said. "Take

bike rides and walks up into the hills. And when it's spring, we'll have a croquet set on the lawn. And we'll go on picnics."

The children looked at their parents with wide dark eyes. And after a moment the boy said, "That will be nice."

"Yes," said the girl. "Nice."

The mother and father glanced at each other, and then the father leaned over and cupped a hand under the boy's chin.

"You know now, don't you, that you did not really see and speak to the people in the books. They were only here in your imagination. You did not *see* the Lilliputians or *talk* to the Red Queen. You did not *see* the cave dwellers or *watch* the tiger eat one of them. They were not *here* in this room. You know that now, don't you?"

The boy looked steadily into his father's eyes.

"Yes," he said, "I know."

The girl nodded her head when the father turned to her. "We know," she said.

"Imagination is a wonderful thing," the father said to both of them. "But it has to be watched, or like a fire, it can get out of control. You'll remember that, won't you?"

"Yes," the boy said, and again the girl nodded, her long hair gleaming in the light.

The father smiled and got to his feet. The mother rose too and smoothed the blankets on both beds. Then they each kissed the children good night with little murmurs of love and reassurance.

"Tomorrow," the father said, "we'll make some plans."

"Yes," the children said, and closed their eyes.

After the mother and father were gone and the room was dark, the children lay still for what seemed to them a long time. The wind rattled the windows, and beyond the hills the moon began to rise.

At last the girl turned to her brother. "Is it time?" she asked.

The boy didn't answer. Instead, he threw back his blanket and crossed the room to the windows. Below, the fields were silvered by the moon, but the hills were a black hulk against the sky.

"Anything could come down from there," he said. "Anything."

The girl came to stand beside him, and together they looked out into the night and thought about the thing waiting outside.

Then the girl said, "Will you take them the book now?"

"Yes," the boy said.

He turned from the windows and went to the dresser. Kneeling on the floor, he pulled open a bottom drawer and felt carefully beneath the socks and undershirts. The girl came over and knelt beside him. Their white faces flowered in the darkness of the room.

They both smiled when the boy took the book out of its hiding place. They rose from the floor, and the boy clasped the book in his arms. He said, "Don't start until I get back."

"Oh, I won't," the girl said. "I wouldn't."

Still holding the book close, the boy went to the door of the room, opened it softly, and stepped out into the hall.

It was a large house and very old, and deep inside it the wind was only a whisper of sound. The boy listened for a moment, then started down the stairs. The carpet was thick under his bare feet, and the railing felt as cold as stone beneath his hand.

Downstairs, a faint spicy smell from the day's baking still lingered in the air. He walked to the back of the house, past dark rooms where mirrors winked from the light in the hall, and night lay thick across the floors.

The mother and father were in the room next to the kitchen. There was a fire in a small grate and empty coffee cups on a table. On the walls were photographs of the children. They looked out into the room with secret smiles.

The mother was seated on the sofa near a shaded lamp. Her lap was full of pink yarn and her knitting needles flashed in the firelight.

The father leaned back in a big leather chair, his eyes on the ceiling, his fingers curled around the bowl of his favorite pipe.

The fire sighed and sparks rose up the chimney. The boy's eyes flicked to the corners of the room where the shadows had retreated from the firelight.

From the doorway he said, "I couldn't sleep until I brought you this." And he went into the room toward his parents, holding the book out to them.

67

"I hid it, but that wasn't right, was it?"

They came to him then. His mother took him into her arms and kissed him, and his father said that he was a fine honest boy.

The mother held him in her lap for a few minutes and warmed his feet with her hands, and her eyes glistened in the light of the fire. They spoke softly to him for a time and he listened and answered "yes" and "no" at the right times, and then he yawned and said that he was sleepy and could he please go back to bed?

They took him to the stairs and kissed him, and he went up alone without looking back.

In the room at the top of the house the girl was waiting for him. He nodded his head, and then they climbed into their beds and joined hands across the narrow space between. Moonlight lay on the floor in cold slabs, and the wind now washed against the windows with a shushing sound.

"Now," the boy said, gripping the girl's hand tightly. "And, remember, it's harder when the book is somewhere else."

They did not move for a long time. Their eyes stared at the ceiling without blinking. Sweat began to glisten on their faces, and their breathing grew short and labored. The room flowed around them. Shadow and light merged and parted like streams in the sea.

When the sounds from below began to reach them, they still did not move. Their joined hands, slick with sweat, held firm. Their muscles strained and corded. Their eyes burned and swam with the shifting light and darkness.

At last the sounds from the bottom of the house stopped. Silence fell around them, cooling their faces, soothing their feverish eyes.

The boy listened and then said, "It's done. You know what to do now, don't you?"

"Yes," the girl said. She slid her hand out of his, brushed her hair back from her face, and closed her eyes. She smiled and thought of a garden filled with flowers. There was a table in the center of the garden, and on the table were china plates. Each plate held a rainbow of iced cakes. There were pink ones and yellow ones and some thick with chocolate. Her tongue flicked over her lips as she thought of how sweet they would taste.

The boy thought of ships—tall ships with white sails. He brought a warm wind out of the south and sent the ships tossing on a sea that was both blue and green. Waves foamed over the decks and the sailors slipped and laughed, while above their heads gulls wheeled in the sky, their wings flashing in the sun.

At the time agreed upon, just as the windows began to lighten, the children rose from their beds and went downstairs.

The house was very cold. The shadows were turning to gray, and in the room next to the kitchen the fire was dead, its coals turned to feathery ash.

The mother lay in a corner of the room, near the outside

wall. The father was a few feet away. He still held the fire-place poker in his hand.

The boy's eyes moved over the room quickly. "I'll find the book," he said. "You go open the door to the terrace."

"Why that one?"

The boy gave her a hard look. "Because that's the one with the catch that slips. It had to get in some way, didn't it?"

The girl turned, then she looked back and said, "Then can we have breakfast?"

The boy had begun moving around the room, looking under tables, poking under the sofa. "There's no time," he said.

"But I'm hungry!"

"I don't care," the boy said. "It's the cleaning lady's day, and we have to be asleep when she gets here. We'll eat later."

"Maybe pancakes? With syrup?"

The boy didn't look at her. "Maybe," he said. "Now go open the door like I told you."

The girl stuck her tongue out at him. "I wish I was the oldest," she said.

"Well, you're not," the boy said, turning and glaring at her. "Now go and do like I said."

The girl tossed her hair back in a gesture of defiance, but she left the room, not hurrying, and in the hall she began to hum a little tune to annoy him.

The boy did not notice. He was becoming anxious now. Where could the book be? It wasn't on the table. And it couldn't be out of the room. He saw it then, on the floor, under the shattered lamp.

He hurried to it and his hands were shaking when he picked it up, brushing the bits of glass away. He examined it carefully, turning the pages, running his fingers over the smooth binding, the embossed letters of that title. Then he smiled. It was all right. There weren't even any spatters of blood.

He closed the covers and hugged the book to his chest. A great joy welled inside him. It was one of his favorite stories. Very soon, he promised himself, he would read *The Hound of the Baskervilles* again.

Red as Blood

by Tanith Lee

A fairy tale! A fairy tale! And finally one with bite.

The beautiful Witch Queen flung open the ivory case of
the magic mirror. Of dark gold the mirror was, dark gold
as the hair of the Witch Queen that poured down her back.
Dark gold the mirror was, and ancient as the seven stunted
black trees growing beyond the pale blue glass of the window.

"*Speculum, speculum,*" said the Witch Queen to the
magic mirror. "*Dei gratia.*"

"*Volente Deo. Audio.*"

"Mirror," said the Witch Queen. "Whom do you
see?"

"I see you, mistress," replied the mirror. "And all in
the land. But one."

"Mirror, mirror, who is it you do not see?"

Red as Blood

"I do not see Bianca."

The Witch Queen crossed herself. She shut the case of the mirror and, walking slowly to the window, looked out at the old trees through the panes of pale blue glass.

Fourteen years ago, another woman had stood at this window, but she was not like the Witch Queen. The woman had black hair that fell to her ankles; she had a crimson gown, the girdle worn high beneath her breasts, for she was far gone with child. And this woman had thrust open the glass casement on the winter garden, where the old trees crouched in the snow. Then, taking a sharp bone needle, she had thrust it into her finger and shaken three bright drops on the ground. "Let my daughter have," said the woman, "hair black as mine, black as the wood of these warped and arcane trees. Let her have skin like mine, white as this snow. And let her have my mouth, red as my blood." And the woman had smiled and licked at her finger. She had a crown on her head; it shone in the dusk like a star. She never came to the window before dusk; she did not like the day. She was the first Queen, and she did not possess a mirror.

The second Queen, the Witch Queen, knew all this. She knew how, in giving birth, the first Queen had died. Her coffin had been carried into the cathedral and masses had been said. There was an ugly rumor—that a splash of holy water had fallen on the corpse and the dead flesh had smoked. But the first Queen had been reckoned unlucky for the kingdom. There had been a strange plague in the land since she came there, a wasting disease for which there was no cure.

Seven years went by. The King married the second Queen, as unlike the first as frankincense to myrrh.

"And this is my daughter," said the King to his second Queen.

There stood a little girl child, nearly seven years of age. Her black hair hung to her ankles, her skin was white as snow. Her mouth was red as blood, and she smiled with it.

"Bianca," said the King, "you must love your new mother."

Bianca smiled radiantly. Her teeth were bright as sharp bone needles.

"Come," said the Witch Queen, "come, Bianca. I will show you my magic mirror."

"Please, Mama," said Bianca softly, "I do not like mirrors."

"She is modest," said the King. "And delicate. She never goes out by day. The sun distresses her."

That night, the Witch Queen opened the case of her mirror.

"Mirror, whom do you see?"

"I see you, mistress. And all in the land. But one."

"Mirror, mirror, who is it you do not see?"

"I do not see Bianca."

The second Queen gave Bianca a tiny crucifix of golden

filigree. Bianca would not accept it. She ran to her father and whispered: "I am afraid. I do not like to think of Our Lord dying in agony on His cross. She means to frighten me. Tell her to take it away."

The second Queen grew wild white roses in her garden and invited Bianca to walk there after sundown. But Bianca shrank away. She whispered to her father: "The thorns will tear me. She means me to be hurt."

When Bianca was twelve years old, the Witch Queen said to the King, "Bianca should be confirmed so that she may take Communion with us."

"This may not be," said the King. "I will tell you, she has not even been christened, for the dying word of my first wife was against it. She begged me, for her religion was different from ours. The wishes of the dying must be respected."

"Should you not like to be blessed by the church," said the Witch Queen to Bianca. "To kneel at the golden rail before the marble altar. To sing to God, to taste the ritual bread and sip the ritual wine."

"She means me to betray my true mother," said Bianca to the King. "When will she cease tormenting me?"

The day she was thirteen, Bianca rose from her bed, and there was a red stain there, like a red, red flower.

"Now you are a woman," said her nurse.

"Yes," said Bianca. And she went to her true mother's jewel box, and out of it she took her mother's crown and set it on her head.

When she walked under the old black trees in the dusk, the crown shone like a star.

The wasting sickness, which had left the land in peace for thirteen years, suddenly began again, and there was no cure.

The Witch Queen sat in a tall chair before a window of pale green and dark white glass, and in her hands she held a Bible bound in rosy silk.

"Majesty," said the huntsman, bowing very low.

He was a man, forty years old, strong and handsome, and wise in the hidden lore of the forests, the occult lore of the earth. He would kill too, for it was his trade, without faltering. The slender fragile deer he could kill, and the moonwinged birds, and the velvet hares with their sad, fore-knowing eyes. He pitied them, but pitying, he killed them. Pity could not stop him. It was his trade.

"Look in the garden," said the Witch Queen.

The hunter looked through a dark white pane. The sun had sunk, and a maiden walked under a tree.

"The Princess Bianca," said the huntsman.

"What else?" asked the Witch Queen.

The huntsman crossed himself.

"By Our Lord, Madam, I will not say."

"But you know."

"Who does not?"

"The King does not."

"Or he does."

"Are you a brave man?" asked the Witch Queen.

"In the summer, I have hunted and slain boar. I have slaughtered wolves in winter."

"But are you brave enough?"

"If you command it, Lady," said the huntsman, "I will try my best."

The Witch Queen opened the Bible at a certain place, and out of it she drew a flat silver crucifix, which had been resting against the words: *Thou shalt not be afraid for the terror by night. . . . Nor for the pestilence that walketh in darkness.*

The huntsman kissed the crucifix and put it about his neck, beneath his shirt.

"Approach," said the Witch Queen, "and I will instruct you in what to say."

Presently, the huntsman entered the garden, as the stars were burning up in the sky. He strode to where Bianca stood under a stunted dwarf tree, and he kneeled down.

"Princess," he said. "Pardon me, but I must give you ill tidings."

"Give them then," said the girl, toying with the long stem of a wan, night-growing flower which she had plucked.

"Your stepmother, that accursed, jealous witch, means to have you slain. There is no help for it but you must fly the palace this very night. If you permit, I will guide you to the forest. There are those who will care for you until it may be safe for you to return."

Bianca watched him, but gently, trustingly.

"I will go with you, then," she said.

They went by a secret way out of the garden, through a passage under the ground, through a tangled orchard, by a broken road between great overgrown hedges.

Night was a pulse of deep, flickering blue when they came to the forest. The branches of the forest overlapped and intertwined like leading in a window, and the sky gleamed dimly through like panes of blue-colored glass.

"I am weary," sighed Bianca. "May I rest a moment?"

"By all means," said the huntsman. "In the clearing there, foxes come to play by night. Look in that direction, and you will see them."

"How clever you are," said Bianca. "And how handsome."

She sat on the turf, and gazed at the clearing.

The huntsman drew his knife silently and concealed it in the folds of his cloak. He stopped above the maiden.

"What are you whispering?" demanded the huntsman, laying his hand on her wood-black hair.

"Only a rhyme my mother taught me."

The huntsman seized her by the hair and swung her about so her white throat was before him, stretched ready for the knife. But he did not strike, for there in his hand he held the dark golden locks of the Witch Queen, and her face laughed up at him and she flung her arms about him, laughing.

"Good man, sweet man, it was only a test of you. Am I not a witch? And do you not love me?"

The huntsman trembled, for he did love her, and she was pressed so close her heart seemed to beat within his own body.

"Put away the knife. Throw away the silly crucifix. We have no need of these things. The King is not one half the man you are."

And the huntsman obeyed her, throwing the knife and the crucifix far off among the roots of the trees. He gripped her to him, and she buried her face in his neck, and the pain of her kiss was the last thing he felt in this world.

The sky was black now. The forest was blacker. No foxes played in the clearing. The moon rose and made white lace through the boughs, and through the backs of the huntsman's empty eyes. Bianca wiped her mouth on a dead flower.

"Seven asleep, seven awake," said Bianca. "Wood to wood. Blood to blood. Thee to me."

There came a sound like seven huge rendings, distant by the length of several trees, a broken road, an orchard, an underground passage. Then a sound like seven huge single footfalls. Nearer. And nearer.

Hop, hop, hop, hop. Hop, hop, hop.

In the orchard, seven black shudderings.

On the broken road, between the high hedges, seven black creepings.

Brush crackled, branches snapped.

Through the forest, into the clearing, pushed seven warped, misshapen, hunched-over, stunted things. Woody-black mossy fur, woody-black bald masks. Eyes like glittering cracks, mouths like moist caverns. Lichen beards. Fingers of twiggy gristle. Grinning. Kneeling. Faces pressed to the earth.

"Welcome," said Bianca.

The Witch Queen stood before a window of glass like diluted wine. She looked at the magic mirror.

"Mirror. Whom do you see?"

"I see you, mistress. I see a man in the forest. He went hunting, but not for deer. His eyes are open, but he is dead. I see all in the land. But one."

The Witch Queen pressed her palms to her ears.

Outside the window the garden lay, empty of its seven black and stunted dwarf trees.

"Bianca," said the Queen.

The windows had been draped and gave no light. The light spilled from a shallow vessel, light in a sheaf, like the pastel wheat. It glowed upon four swords that pointed east and west, that pointed north and south.

Four winds had burst through the chamber, and three arch-winds. Cool fires had risen, and parched oceans, and the gray-silver powders of Time.

The hands of the Witch Queen floated like folded leaves on the air, and through dry lips the Witch Queen chanted.

"Pater omnipotens, mittere digneris sanctum Angelum tuum de Infernis."

The light faded, and grew brighter.

There, between the hilts of the four swords, stood the Angel Lucefiel, somberly gilded, his face in shadow, his golden wings spread and blazing at his back.

"Since you have called me, I know your desire. It is a comfortless wish. You ask for pain."

"You speak of pain, Lord Lucefiel, who suffer the most merciless pain of all. Worse than the nails in the feet and wrists. Worse than the thorns and the bitter cup and the blade in the side. To be called upon for evil's sake, which I do not, comprehending your true nature, son of God, brother of The Son."

"You recognize me, then. I will grant what you ask."

And Lucefiel (by some named Satan, Rex Mundi, but nevertheless the left hand, the sinister hand of God's design) wrenched lightning from the ether and cast it at the Witch Queen.

It caught her in the breast. She fell.

The sheaf of light towered and lit the golden eyes of the Angel, which were terrible, yet luminous with compassion, as the swords shattered and he vanished.

The Witch Queen pulled herself from the floor of the chamber, no longer beautiful, a withered, slobbering hag.

Into the core of the forest, even at noon, the sun never shone. Flowers propagated in the grass, but they were colorless. Above, the black-green roof hung down nets of thick, green twilight through which albino butterflies and moths feverishly drizzled. The trunks of the trees were smooth as the stalks of underwater weeds. Bats flew in the daytime, and birds who believed themselves to be bats.

There was a sepulcher, dripped with moss. The bones had been rolled out, had rolled around the feet of seven twisted dwarf trees. They looked like trees. Sometimes they moved. Sometimes something like an eye glittered, or a tooth, in the wet shadows.

In the shade of the sepulcher door sat Bianca, combing her hair.

A lurch of motion disturbed the thick twilight.

The seven trees turned their heads.

A hag emerged from the forest. She was crook-backed and her head was poked forward, predatory, withered, and almost hairless, like a vulture's.

"Here we are at last," grated the hag, in a vulture's voice.

She came closer, and cranked herself down on her knees, and bowed her face into the turf and the colorless flowers.

Bianca sat and gazed at her. The hag lifted herself. Her teeth were yellow palings.

"I bring you the homage of witches, and three gifts," said the hag.

"Why should you do that?"

"Such a quick child, and only fourteen years. Why? Because we fear you. I bring you gifts to curry favor."

Bianca laughed. "Show me."

The hag made a pass in the green air. She held a silken

cord worked curiously with plaited human hair.

"Here is a girdle which will protect you from the devices of priests, from crucifix and chalice and the accursed holy water. In it are knotted the tresses of a virgin, and of a woman no better than she should be, and of a woman dead. And here—" a second pass and a comb was in her hand, lacquered blue over green—"a comb from the deep sea, a mermaid's trinket, to charm and subdue. Part your locks with this, and the scent of ocean will fill men's nostrils and the rhythm of the tides their ears, the tides that bind men like chains. Last," added the hag, "that old symbol of wickedness, the scarlet fruit of Eve, the apple red as blood. Bite, and the understanding of sin, which the serpent boasted of, will be made known to you." And the hag made her last pass in the air and extended the apple, with the girdle and the comb, toward Bianca.

Bianca glanced at the seven stunted trees.

"I like her gifts, but I do not quite trust her."

The bald masks peered from their shaggy beardings. Eyelets glinted. Twiggy claws clacked.

"All the same," said Bianca. "I will let her tie the girdle on me, and comb my hair herself."

The hag obeyed, simpering. Like a toad she waddled to Bianca. She tied on the girdle. She parted the ebony hair. Sparks sizzled, white from the girdle, peacock's eye from the comb.

"And now, hag, take a little bite of the apple."

"It will be my pride," said the hag, "to tell my sisters I

shared this fruit with you." And the hag bit into the apple, and mumbled the bite noisily, and swallowed, smacking her lips.

Then Bianca took the apple and bit into it.

Bianca screamed—and choked.

She jumped to her feet. Her hair whirled about her like a storm cloud. Her face turned blue, then slate, then white again. She lay on the pallid flowers, neither stirring nor breathing.

The seven dwarf trees rattled their limbs and their bear-shaggy heads, to no avail. Without Bianca's art they could not hop. They strained their claws and ripped at the hag's sparse hair and her mantle. She fled between them. She fled into the sunlit acres of the forest, along the broken road, through the orchard, into a hidden passage.

The hag reentered the palace by the hidden way, and the Queen's chamber by a hidden stair. She was bent almost double. She held her ribs. With one skinny hand she opened the ivory case of the magic mirror.

"*Speculum, speculum. Dei gratia.* Whom do you see?"

"I see you, mistress. And all in the land. And I see a coffin."

"Whose corpse lies in the coffin?"

"That I cannot see. It must be Bianca."

The hag, who had been the beautiful Witch Queen, sank into her tall chair before the window of pale, cucumber green and dark white glass. Her drugs and potions waited, ready to reverse the dreadful conjuring of age the Angel Lucefiel had placed on her, but she did not touch them yet.

The apple had contained a fragment of the flesh of Christ, the sacred wafer, the Eucharist.

The Witch Queen drew her Bible to her and opened it randomly.

And read, with fear, the word: *Resurcat.*

It appeared like glass, the coffin, milky glass. It had formed this way. A thin white smoke had risen from the skin of Bianca. She smoked as a fire smokes when a drop of quenching water falls on it. The piece of Eucharist had stuck in her throat. The Eucharist, quenching water to her fire, caused her to smoke.

Then the cold dews of night gathered, and the colder atmospheres of midnight. The smoke of Bianca's quenching froze about her. Frost formed in exquisite silver scroll-work all over the block of misty ice that contained Bianca.

Bianca's frigid heart could not warm the ice. Nor the sunless, green twilight of the day.

You could just see her, stretched in the coffin, through the glass. How lovely she looked, Bianca. Black as ebony, white as snow, red as blood.

The trees hung over the coffin. Years passed. The trees sprawled about the coffin, cradling it in their arms. Their eyes wept fungus and green resin. Green amber drops hardened like jewels in the coffin of glass.

"Who is that lying under the trees?" the Prince asked, as he rode into the clearing.

He seemed to bring a golden moon with him, shining about his golden head, on the golden armor and the cloak of white satin blazoned with gold and blood and ink and sapphire. The white horse trod on the colorless flowers, but the flowers sprang up again when the hoofs had passed. A shield hung from the saddle-bow, a strange shield. From one side it had a lion's face, but from the other, a lamb's face.

The trees groaned, and their heads split on huge mouths.

"Is this Bianca's coffin?" asked the Prince.

"Leave her with us," said the seven trees. They hauled at their roots. The ground shivered. The coffin of ice-glass gave a great jolt, and a crack bisected it.

Bianca coughed.

The jolt had precipitated the piece of Eucharist from her throat.

Into a thousand shards the coffin shattered, and Bianca sat up. She stared at the Prince, and she smiled.

"Welcome, beloved," said Bianca.

She got to her feet, and shook out her hair, and began to walk toward the Prince on the pale horse.

But she seemed to walk into a shadow, into a purple room, then into a crimson room whose emanations lanced her like knives. Next she walked into a yellow room where she heard the sound of crying, which tore her ears. All her body seemed stripped away; she was a beating heart. The beats of her heart became two wings. She flew. She was a raven, then an owl. She flew into a sparkling pane. It scorched her white. Snow white. She was a dove.

She settled on the shoulder of the Prince and hid her head under her wing. She had no longer anything black about her, and nothing red.

"Begin again now, Bianca," said the Prince. He raised her from his shoulder. On his wrist there was a mark. It was like a star. Once a nail had been driven in there.

Bianca flew away, up through the roof of the forest. She flew in at a delicate wine window. She was in the palace. She was seven years old.

The Witch Queen, her new mother, hung a filigree crucifix around her neck.

"Mirror," said the Witch Queen. "Whom do you see?"

"I see you, mistress," replied the mirror. "And all in the land. I see Bianca."

Gabriel-Ernest

by Saki (H. H. Munro)

It's sad but true that what is not believed is seldom seen.

"There is a wild beast in your woods," said the artist Cunningham, as he was being driven to the station. It was the only remark he had made during the drive, but as Van Cheele had talked incessantly, his companion's silence had not been noticeable.

"A stray fox or two and some resident weasels. Nothing more formidable," said Van Cheele. The artist said nothing.

"What did you mean about a wild beast?" said Van Cheele later, when they were on the platform.

"Nothing. My imagination. Here is the train," said Cunningham.

That afternoon Van Cheele went for one of his frequent rambles through his woodland property. He had a stuffed bittern in his study and knew the names of quite a number of wild flowers, so his aunt had possibly some justification in describing him as a great naturalist. At any rate, he was a great walker. It was his custom to take mental notes of everything he saw during his walks, not so much for the purpose of assisting contemporary science as to provide topics for conversation afterwards. When the bluebells began to show themselves in flower, he made a point of informing everyone of the fact; the season of the year might have warned his hearers of the likelihood of such an occurrence, but at least they felt that he was being absolutely frank with them.

What Van Cheele saw on this particular afternoon was, however, something far removed from his ordinary range of experience. On a shelf of smooth stone overhanging a deep pool in the hollow of an oak coppice, a boy of about sixteen lay asprawl, drying his wet brown limbs luxuriously in the sun. His wet hair, parted by a recent dive, lay close to his head, and his light-brown eyes, so light that there was an almost tigerish gleam in them, were turned toward Van Cheele with a certain lazy watchfulness. It was an unexpected apparition, and Van Cheele found himself engaged in the novel process of thinking before he spoke. Where on earth could this wild-looking boy hail from? The miller's wife had lost a child some two months ago, supposed to have been swept away by the millrace, but that had been a mere baby, not a half-grown lad.

"What are you doing there?" he demanded.

"Obviously, sunning myself," replied the boy.

"Where do you live?"

"Here, in these woods."

"You can't live in the woods," said Van Cheele.

"They are very nice woods," said the boy, with a touch of patronage in his voice.

"But where do you sleep at night?"

"I don't sleep at night; that's my busiest time."

Van Cheele began to have an irritated feeling that he was grappling with a problem that was eluding him.

"What do you feed on?" he asked.

"Flesh," said the boy, and he pronounced the word with slow relish, as though he were tasting it.

"Flesh! What flesh?"

"Since it interests you, rabbits, wild-fowl, hares, poultry, lambs in their season, children when I can get any; they're usually too well locked in at night, when I do most of my hunting. It's quite two months since I tasted child-flesh."

Ignoring the chaffing nature of the last remark, Van Cheele tried to draw the boy onto the subject of possible poaching operations.

"You're talking rather through your hat when you speak of feeding on hares." (Considering the nature of the boy's toilet, the simile was hardly an apt one.) "Our hillside hares aren't easily caught."

"At night I hunt on four feet" was the somewhat cryptic response.

"I suppose you mean that you hunt with a dog?" hazarded Van Cheele.

The boy rolled slowly over onto his back and laughed a weird low laugh that was pleasantly like a chuckle and disagreeably like a snarl.

"I don't fancy any dog would be very anxious for my company, especially at night."

Van Cheele began to feel that there was something positively uncanny about the strange-eyed, strange-tongued youngster.

"I can't have you staying in these woods," he declared authoritatively.

"I fancy you'd rather have me here than in your house," said the boy.

The prospect of this wild, nude animal in Van Cheele's primly ordered house was certainly an alarming one.

"If you don't go, I shall have to make you," said Van Cheele.

The boy turned like a flash, plunged into the pool, and in a moment had flung his wet and glistening body halfway up the bank where Van Cheele was standing. In an otter the movement would not have been remarkable; in a boy Van Cheele found it sufficiently startling. His foot slipped as he made an involuntary backward movement, and he found himself almost prostrate on the slippery weed-grown bank, with those tigerish yellow eyes not very far from his own. Almost instinctively he half-raised his hand to his throat. The boy laughed again, a laugh in which the snarl had nearly driven out the chuckle, and then, with another of his astonishing lightning movements, plunged out of view into a yielding tangle of weed and fern.

"What an extraordinary wild animal!" said Van Cheele as he picked himself up. And then he recalled Cunningham's remark, "There is a wild beast in your woods."

Walking slowly homeward, Van Cheele began to turn over in his mind various local occurrences which might be traceable to the existence of this astonishing young savage.

Something had been thinning the game in the woods lately, poultry had been missing from the farms, hares were growing unaccountably scarcer, and complaints had reached him of lambs being carried off bodily from the hills. Was it possible that this wild boy was really hunting the countryside in company with some clever poacher dog? He had spoken of hunting "four-footed" by night, but then again, he had hinted strangely at no dog caring to come near him, "especially at night." It was certainly puzzling. And then, as Van Cheele ran his mind over the various depredations that had been committed during the last month or two, he came suddenly to a dead stop, alike in his walk and his speculations. The child missing from the mill two months ago—the accepted theory was that it had tumbled into the millrace and been swept away; but the mother had always declared she had heard a shriek on the hill side of the house, in the opposite direction from the water. It was unthinkable, of course, but he wished that the boy had not made that uncanny remark about child-flesh eaten two months ago. Such dreadful things should not be said even in fun.

Van Cheele, contrary to his usual wont, did not feel disposed to be communicative about his discovery in the wood. His position as a parish councillor and justice of the peace seemed somehow compromised by the fact that he was harboring a personality of such doubtful repute on his property; there was even a possibility that a heavy bill of damages for raided lambs and poultry might be laid at his door. At dinner that night he was quite unusually silent.

"Where's your voice gone to?" said his aunt. "One would think you had seen a wolf."

Van Cheele, who was not familiar with the old saying, thought the remark rather foolish; if he *had* seen a wolf on his property, his tongue would have been extraordinarily busy with the subject.

At breakfast next morning Van Cheele was conscious that his feeling of uneasiness regarding yesterday's episode had not wholly disappeared, and he resolved to go by train to the neighboring cathedral town, hunt up Cunningham, and learn from him what he had really seen that had prompted the remark about a wild beast in the woods. With this resolution taken, his usual cheerfulness partially returned, and he hummed a bright little melody as he sauntered to the morning room for his customary cigarette. As he entered the room, the melody made way abruptly for a pious invocation. Gracefully asprawl on the ottoman, in an attitude of almost exaggerated repose, was the boy of the woods. He was drier than when Van Cheele had last seen him, but no other alteration was noticeable in his toilet.

"How dare you come here?" asked Van Cheele furiously.

"You told me I was not to stay in the woods," said the boy calmly.

93

"But not to come here. Supposing my aunt should see you!"

And with a view to minimizing that catastrophe Van Cheele hastily obscured as much of his unwelcome guest as possible under the folds of a *Morning Post*. At that moment his aunt entered the room.

"This is a poor boy who has lost his way—and lost his memory. He doesn't know who he is or where he comes from," explained Van Cheele desperately, glancing apprehensively at the waif's face to see whether he was going to add inconvenient candor to his other savage propensities.

Miss Van Cheele was enormously interested.

"Perhaps his underlinen is marked," she suggested.

"He seems to have lost most of that, too," said Van Cheele, making frantic little grabs at the *Morning Post* to keep it in its place.

A naked, homeless child appealed to Miss Van Cheele as warmly as a stray kitten or derelict puppy would have.

"We must do all we can for him," she decided; and in a very short time a messenger, dispatched to the rectory, where a page-boy was kept, had returned with a suit of pantry clothes, and the necessary accessories of shirt, shoes, collar, etc. Clothed, clean and groomed, the boy lost none of his uncanniness in Van Cheele's eyes, but his aunt found him sweet.

"We must call him something till we know who he really is," she said. "Gabriel-Ernest, I think; those are nice suitable names."

Van Cheele agreed, but he privately doubted whether they were being grafted on to a nice suitable child. His misgivings were not diminished by the fact that his staid and elderly spaniel had bolted out of the house at the first incoming of the boy and now obstinately remained shivering and yapping at the farther end of the orchard, while the canary, usually as vocally industrious as Van Cheele himself, had put itself on an allowance of frightened cheeps. More than ever he was resolved to consult Cunningham without loss of time.

As he drove off to the station, his aunt was arranging that Gabriel-Ernest should help her to entertain the infant members of her Sunday-school class at tea that afternoon.

Cunningham was not at first disposed to be communicative.

"My mother died of some brain trouble," he explained, "so you will understand why I am averse to dwelling on anything of an impossibly fantastic nature that I may see or think that I have seen."

"But what *did* you see?" persisted Van Cheele.

"What I thought I saw was something so extraordinary that no really sane man could dignify it with the credit of having actually happened. I was standing, the last evening I was with you, half-hidden in the hedgegrowth by the orchard gate, watching the dying glow of the sunset. Suddenly I became aware of a naked boy, a bather from some neighboring pool, I took him to be, who was standing out on the bare hillside also watching the sunset. His pose was so suggestive of some wild faun of Pagan myth that I instantly wanted to engage him as a model, and in another moment I think I should have hailed him. But just then the sun dipped out of view, and all the orange and pink slid out of the landscape, leaving it cold and gray. And at the same moment an astounding thing happened—the boy vanished too!"

"What! Vanished away into nothing?" asked Van Cheele excitedly.

"No, that is the dreadful part of it," answered the artist. "On the open hillside where the boy had been standing a second ago, stood a large wolf, blackish in color, with gleaming fangs and cruel, yellow eyes. You may think—"

But Van Cheele did not stop for anything as futile as thought. Already he was tearing at top speed toward the station. He dismissed the idea of a telegram. "Gabriel-Ernest is a werewolf" was a hopelessly inadequate effort at conveying the situation, and his aunt would think it was a code message to which he had omitted to give her the key. His one hope was that he might reach home before sundown. The cab that he chartered at the other end of the railway journey bore him with what seemed exasperating slowness along the country roads, which were pink and mauve with the flush of the sinking sun. His aunt was putting away some unfinished jams and cake when he arrived.

"Where is Gabriel-Ernest?" he almost screamed.

"He is taking the little Toop child home," said his aunt. "It was getting so late, I thought it wasn't safe to let him go back alone. What a lovely sunset, isn't it?"

But Van Cheele, although not oblivious of the glow in the western sky, did not stay to discuss its beauties. At a speed for which he was scarcely geared, he raced along the narrow lane that led to the home of the Toops. On one side ran the swift current of the millstream, on the other rose the stretch of bare hillside. A dwindling rim of red sun showed still on the skyline, and the next turning must bring him in view of the ill-assorted couple he was pursuing. Then the color went suddenly out of things, and a gray light settled itself with a quick shiver over the landscape. Van Cheele heard a shrill wail of fear and stopped running.

Nothing was ever seen again of the Toops' child or Gabriel-Ernest, but the latter's discarded garments were found lying in the road, so it was assumed that the child had fallen into the water, and that the boy had stripped and jumped in, in a vain endeavor to save him. Van Cheele and some workmen who were nearby at the time testified to having heard a child scream loudly just near the spot where the clothes were found. Mrs. Toop, who had eleven other children, was decently resigned to her bereavement, but Miss Van Cheele sincerely mourned her lost foundling. It was on her initiative that a memorial brass was put up in the parish church to "Gabriel-Ernest, an unknown boy, who bravely sacrificed his life for another."

Van Cheele gave way to his aunt in most things, but he flatly refused to subscribe to the Gabriel-Ernest memorial.

Fritzchen

by Charles Beaumont

Only after a few days did the little monster's problems become apparent.

It had once been a place for dreaming. For lying on your back in the warm sand and listening to the silence and making faraway things seem real. The finest place in all the world for all the reasons that ever were.

But it had stopped being this long ago. Now, he supposed, it wasn't much more than a fairly isolated cove, really; a stretch of land bleeding into the river at one of its wide points, cut off like a tiny peninsula; a grey, dull place, damp and unnatural from its nights beneath the tidewaters—decaying, sinking slowly, glad to be eaten by the river. As Edna had put it: Just a lot of dirty wet sand. Not a place for dreaming anymore.

Mr. Peldo shifted his position and sighed as he remembered. He took from his mouth the eviscerated end of a lifeless cigar, flipped it away distastefully, watched as the mud whitened and oozed where it landed, and the spiders lumbered clumsily away in fright.

The spiders made him think of his snakes. And soon he was thinking, too, of rabbits and goldfish and ooo wow-wow puppy dogs, all flop-eared and soft, common as a blade of grass—and his bread-and-butter. His living.

He was almost relieved to hear Edna's coarse voice beside him.

"Jake."

She would now make some complaint about the foolishness of this whole trip, adding that it made her sinuses runny.

"Yes, Chicken, what is it?"

"Go and see to Luther."

Go-and-see-to-Luther. Eight-year-old kid ought to be able to see to himself, by God.

"All right. Where'd he go?"

"Somewhere over in that direction, there by the trees. I'm worried he might think of going in the water or get lost."

Mr. Peldo grunted softly as he pulled his weight erect. Exertion. Oh well, that was all right. Soon he would have started with the frustration, thinking about the lousy pet shop and his lousy life. Better to hunt in the trees for spoiled brats.

It was hard going. Had to end in a few yards, of course, but still, it *was* . . . exciting, in a small, tired, remembering way. He pushed aside a drenched fern, and another, needles of wet hitting him.

"Luther."

Mr. Peldo continued for a few feet, until he could distinctly hear the current. A wall of leaves rose at the curve, so he stopped there, let the last of the thrill fall loose from him, then listened.

"Luther. Hustle, boy."

Only the water. The vibrant, treacherous river water, hurrying to join the Sound and to go with it to the ocean.

"Hey, *Luu-therr.*"

Mr. Peldo stabbed his hands into the foliage and parted it. From the window, by peering close, he could see his son's back.

"Boy, when your father calls you, *answer* him, hear!"

Luther looked around disinterestedly, frowned and turned his head. He was sitting in the mud, playing.

Mr. Peldo felt the anger course spastically through him. He pushed forward and stopped, glared.

"Well?"

Then he glimpsed what his son had been playing with. Only a glimpse, though.

"Fritzchen!" Luther pronounced defiantly, shielding something in his hands. "Fritzchen—like I wanted to call Sol's birdie."

Mr. Peldo felt his eyes smart and rubbed them. "What have you got there?"

"Fritzchen, Fritzchen," the boy wailed. There was another sound then. A sound like none Mr. Peldo had ever heard: high-pitched, whiny, discordant. The sound an animal makes when it is in pain.

Mr. Peldo reached down and slapped at his son's mouth, which had fastened like a python's about the calf of his left leg. Then, by holding his thumb and forefinger tightly on Luther's nose, he forced him to drop the thing he had been hiding.

It fell onto the slime and began to thrash.

Mr. Peldo gasped. He stared for a moment, like an idiot at a lampshade, his mouth quite open, and his eyes bulged.

A thin voice from across the trees called: "Jake, is there anything wrong? Answer me!"

He pulled off his sport coat and threw it about the squirmy thing. "No, no, everything's okay. Kid's just acting up is all. Hold your horses!"

"Well, hurry! It's getting dark!"

Mr. Peldo blocked Luther's charge with his foot.

"Where did you get that?"

Luther did not answer. He glowered sullenly at the ground, mumbling, "He's mine. I found him. You can't have him."

"Where did it come from?" Mr. Peldo demanded.

Luther's lower lip resembled a bloated sausage. Finally he jerked his thumb in the direction of the riverbank.

"You can talk!"

Luther whimpered, tried once again to get at the wriggling bundle on the sand, sat down and said, "I found him in the water. I snuck up on him and grabbed him when he wasn't looking. Now he's mine and you can't have—"

But Mr. Peldo, having recovered himself, had plucked off the coat and was staring.

A place for dreaming.

Roadsters that would go over two hundred miles per hour. Promontoried chateaus with ten bathrooms. Coveys of lithe young temptresses, vacant-minded, full-bodied, infinitely imaginative, infinitely accessible . . .

"JAAAAke! Are you trying to scare me to death? It's cold and my sinuses are beginning to run!"

Luther looked at his father, snorted loudly and started for the trees.

"He's Fritzchen and he's *mine!*" he called back as he ran. "All right—I'll get even! You'll see!"

Mr. Peldo watched the small creature, fascinated, as all its legs commenced to move together, dwarfed, undeveloped legs, burrowing into the viscous ground. Shuddering slightly, he replaced the coat, gathered it into the form of a sack and started through the shrubbery.

Edna's nose had turned red. He decided not to show Fritzchen to her, for a while.

"Got no empties," Sol said slowly, eying the bundle Mr. Peldo held at arms' length. Sol didn't care for animals. He was old; his mind had fallen into a ravine; it paced the ravine, turned and paced, like a contented baboon. He was old.

Mr. Peldo waited for Edna and Luther to go around to the living quarters in the back. "Put the capuchin in with Bess," he said. "Ought to have a stout one. Hop to it, Sol, I can't stand here holding this all day."

" 'nother stray?"

"You . . . might say."

Sol shrugged and transferred the raucous little monkey from his carved wood cage to the parrot dome.

Then he looked back. Mr. Peldo was holding the jacket-bundle down on a table with both hands. Whatever was inside was moving in violent spasms, not the way a dog moves or a rabbit. There were tiny sounds.

"Give me a hand," Mr. Peldo said, and Sol helped him put the bundle, jacket and all, into the cage. They locked it.

"This'll do for a while," Mr. Peldo said, "until I can build a proper one. Now mind, Sol, you keep your mouth strictly shut about this. Shut."

Sol didn't answer. His nose had snapped upward and he held a conched hand behind his ear.

"Listen, you," Sol said.

Mr. Peldo took his fingers off the sport coat, which had begun to show a purplish stain.

"First time it ever happened in sixteen years," Sol said.

The silence roared. The silent pet shop roared and burst and pulsed with tension, quiet electric tension. The animals didn't move anywhere in the room. Mr. Peldo's eyes darted from cage to cage, seeing the second strangest thing he had ever seen: unmoving snakes, coiled or supine, but still, as though listening; monkeys hidden in far corners, haunched; rabbits—even their noses quiet and frozen; white mice huddled at the bottom of mills that turned in cautious, diminishing arcs, frightened, staring creatures.

The phlegm in Mr. Peldo's throat racked loose.

Then it was quiet again. Though not exactly quiet.

Sol quit his survey of the animals and turned back to the occupant of the capuchin's cage. The sport jacket glistened with stain now, and from within the dark folds there was a scrabbling and a small gurgling sound.

Then the jacket fell away.

"Tom-hell, Jake!" Sol said.

The animals had begun to scream, all of them, all at once.

"Not a word to anyone now, Sol! Promise."

Mr. Peldo feasted. He stared and stared, feeling satisfaction.

"What in glory is it?" Sol inquired above the din.

"A pet," Mr. Peldo answered, simply.

"Pet, hey?"

"We'll have to build a special cage for it." Mr. Peldo beamed. "Say, bet there ain't many like this one! No, sir. We'll have to read up on it so's we can get the feeding right and all . . ."

"*You* read up." Sol's eyes were large. The air was filled with the wild beating of birds' wings.

Mr. Peldo was musing. "By the way, Sol, what you suppose it could be?"

The old man cocked his head to one side, peered from slitted eyes, picked out the crumpled sport jacket quickly and let it fall to the floor. It dropped heavily and exuded a sick water smell. Sol shrugged.

"Cross between a whale," he said, "and a horsefly, near's I can see."

"Maybe it's valuable—you think?" Mr. Peldo's ideas were growing.

"Couldn't say. Most likely not, in the face of it."

The chittering sound rose into a sort of staccato wail, piercing, clear over the frantic pets.

"Where in thunder you get it?"

"*He* didn't. *I* did." It was Luther, scowling, in his nightclothes.

"Go to bed. Go away."

"I found Fritzchen in the water. He likes me."

"*Out!*"

"Dirty stinking rotten lousy rotten stealer!"

Sol put his fingers into his ears and shut his eyes.

Luther made a pout and advanced toward Fritzchen's cage. The sobbing noises ceased.

"He hadda lock you up. Yeah. *I* was gonna let you loose again." The boy glared at his father. "See how he loves me." Luther put his face up to the cage, and as he did so, the small animal came forward, ponderously, with suction-like noises from its many legs.

Mr. Peldo looked disinterested. He inspected his watch stem. Neither he nor Sol saw what happened.

Luther stamped his foot and yelled. The right side of his face was covered with something that gathered and dripped down.

"Luther!" It was Mr. Peldo's wife. She ran into the room and looked at the cage. "Oh, that nasty thing!" She stormed out, clutching her son's pink ear.

"Damn woman will drive me crazy," Mr. Peldo said. Then he noticed that the shop was quiet again. Sol had thrown the damp jacket over Fritzchen's cage. There was only the sobbing.

"Funny!"

Mr. Peldo bent down, lifted the end of the coat and put his face close. He jerked back with abnormal speed, swabbing at his cheek.

There was a sound like a drowning kitten's purr.

Luther stood in the back doorway. Hate and astonishment contorted his features. "That's all he cares about me when I only wanted to be good to him! Now he loves *you*, dirty rotten—"

"Look, boy, your father's getting mighty tired of—"

"Yeah, well, he'll be sorry."

Fritzchen began to chitter again.

When Mr. Peldo returned to the shop after dinner, he found a curious thing. Bess, the parrot, lay on her side, dead.

Everything else was normal. The animals were wakeful or somnolent but normal. Fritzchen's cage was covered with a canvas, and there was silence from within.

Mr. Peldo inspected Bess and was horrified to discover the bird's condition. She lay inundated in an odd miasmic jelly which had hardened and was now spongey to the touch. It covered her completely. What was more, extended prodding revealed that something had happened to Bess's insides.

They were gone.

And without a trace. Even the bones. Bess was little more than skin and feathers.

Mr. Peldo recalled the substance that had struck his face when he examined Fritzchen's cage the last time. In a frenzy he pulled off the tarpaulin. But Fritzchen was there, and the cage was as securely locked as ever.

And easily twenty feet from the parrot dome.

He went back and found the capuchin staring at him out of quizzical eyes.

Luther, of course. Monster boy. Spoiled bug of a child. He had an active imagination. Probably rigged the whole thing, like the time he emasculated the parakeet in an attempt to turn it inside out.

Mr. Peldo was ungratified that the animals had not yet gotten used to Fritzchen. They began their harangue, so he switched off the light and waited for his eyes to accustom themselves to the moonlight. Moonlight comes fast to small towns near rivers.

Fritzchen must be sleeping. Curled like a baby anaconda, legs slender filaments adhering to the cage floor, the tender tiny tail tucked around so that the tip rested just inside the immense mouth.

Mr. Peldo studied the animal. He watched the mouth especially, noting its outsized relationship to the rest of the body.

But—Mr. Peldo peered—could it actually be that Fritzchen was *larger?* Surely not. The stomach did seem fatter, yet the finely ground hamburger, the dish of milk, the oysters, sat to one side, untouched. Nor had the accommodating bathing and drinking pool been disturbed.

Then he noticed, for the first time, that the mouth had no teeth. There did not appear to be a gullet! And the spiny snout, with its florid green cup, was not a nose after all, for the nose was elsewhere.

But most curious of all, Fritzchen had grown. Oh, yes, grown. No doubt about it.

Mr. Peldo retired hours later with sparkling visions of wealth. He would contact—somebody appropriate—and sell his find for many hundreds of thousands of dollars. Then he would run away to Europe and play with a different woman every night until he died of his excesses.

He was awakened a short time later by Sol, who informed him that the bird of paradise and one dalmatian pup had died during the night. He knew because he'd heard the racket from clean across the street.

"Oh, not the ooo wow-wow," said Edna. "Not the liddle puppy!"

Luther sat up in bed, interested.

"How'd it happen?" Mr. Peldo said.

"Don't know. No good way for definite sure." Sol's eyelids almost closed. "Their innards is gone."

Edna put her head beneath the covers.

"Fritzchen?"

"Guess. Y'ought'a do somethin' with that crittur. Bad actor."

"He got out—that it?"

"Hey-up. Or somebody let him out. Cage is all locked up tight as wax, 'n it wailin' like a banshee."

Mr. Peldo whirled to face his son, who stuck out his tongue.

"See here, young fellow, we're going to get to the bottom of this. If I find out that you—"

"Don't think t'was the lad," Sol said.

"Why not?"

"Wa'l . . . that there thing is thrice the size 'twas yesterday when you brung 'er in."

"No."

"No nothin'. Stomach's pooched out like it's fit to bust."

Mr. Peldo got up and rubbed his hand over his bald head.

"But look, Sol, if it didn't get out, and—Luther, you didn't let it out, did you?"

"No, ma'am."

"—then how we going to blame it? Maybe there's a disease going around."

"*I* know, *I* know," Luther sang, swinging his feet in the air. "His nose can go longer."

"Be still, boy."

"Well, it *can!* I saw it. Fritzchen did it on the beach— hit a bird way out over the water, and he didn't move out of my hands."

"What happened to the bird, Luther?"

"Well, it got stuck up with this stuff Fritzchen has inside him, so it couldn't do anything. Then when it was all glued, Fritzchen pulled it back closer to him and shot out his nose and put his nose inside the bird's mou—"

Mr. Peldo felt his cheek, where the molasses had gathered that time. Both he and Luther had thought of it as an affectionate gesture, no worse than a St. Bernard leaping and pawing over you, raking your face, covering you with friendly, doggy slobber.

That's why Luther had gotten angry.

But Fritzchen wasn't being affectionate. It didn't work only because Fritzchen was too small, or they had been too big.

Mr. Peldo remembered Bess.

Edna poked her head out of the covers and said, "You listen to that! The neighbors will kill us!"

The sounds from the shop were growing stronger and louder and more chaotic.

Mr. Peldo dashed to the hall and returned with a telephone book. "Here," he said, tossing it to his wife, "get the numbers of all the zoos and museums."

"He's mine, he's mine!" Luther screeched.

Sol, who was old, said, "Jake, you never you mind about that. You just fished up something quaar, is all, and the best thing you can do is chuck 'er smack back where she come from."

"Edna—get those numbers, do you hear me? All the museums in the state. I'll be back."

The wailing had reached a crescendo now.

And Luther had disappeared.

Mr. Peldo put on a robe and hurried across the frosty lawn to the back door of the shop.

"Luther!"

The small boy had a box of kitchen matches. Holding a cluster of them in his hands, he lit them and hurled them into Fritzchen's cage. The fiery sticks landed; there was a cry of pain, and then the matches spluttered out against moist skin.

"Luther!"

"I wanted to be good to you," Luther was saying, "but then you hadda take up with *him!* Yeah, well, now you'll see!"

Mr. Peldo threw his son out the door.

The painful wail became an intermittent cry—a strange cry, not unmelodious.

Mr. Peldo looked into the great jeweled milk-white eyes of the creature and dodged as the snout unrolled like a party favor, spraying a fine crystal glaze of puce jam.

Fritzchen stood erect. He—it—had changed. There were antennae where no antennae had been; many of the legs had developed claws; the mouth, which had been toothless the day before, was now filled with sharp brown needles. Fritzchen had been fifteen inches high when Mr. Peldo first saw him. Now he stood over thirty inches.

Still time, though. Time for everything.

Mr. Peldo looked at the animal until his eyes hurt; then he saw the newspaper on the floor. It was soaked with what looked like shreds of liquid soap-jelly, greenish, foul with the odor of seaweed and other things. On it lay a bird and a small dog.

He felt sad for a moment. But then he thought again of some of the things he had dreamed a long time ago, of what he had now, and he determined to make certain telephone calls.

A million dollars, or almost, probably. They'd—oh, they'd stuff Fritzchen, at all odds, or something like that.

"Dirty rotten lousy—"

Luther had come back. He had a crumpled-up magazine saturated with oil and lighter fluid. The magazine was on fire.

The monkeys and the rabbits and the mice and the goldfish and the cats and birds and dogs shrilled in fear. But Fritzchen didn't.

Fritzchen howled only once. Or lowed—a deep sound from somewhere in the middle of his body that seemed to come from his body and not just his mouth. It was an eerily mournful sound that carried a new tone, a tone of helplessness. Then the creature was silent.

By the time Mr. Peldo reached the cage, Luther had thrown in the paper and was squirting inflammable fluid from a can. The fire burned fiercely.

"I *told* you," Luther said, pettishly.

When the fire was pulled and scattered and trampled out, an ugly thing remained in the cage. An ugly blackened thing that made no noise.

Luther began to cry.

Then he stopped.

And Mr. Peldo stopped chasing him.

Sol and Edna, in the doorway, didn't move either.

They all listened.

It could have been a crazed elephant shambling madly through a straw village . . .

Or a whale blind with the pain of sharp steel, thrashing and leaping in illimitable waters . . .

Or it could have been a massive hawk swooping in outraged vengeance upon the killers of her young . . .

The killers of her young!

In that moment, before the rustling sound grew huge; before the windows shattered and the great nightmarish shadow came into the shop, Mr. Peldo understood the meaning of Fritzchen's inconsolable cries.

They were the cries of a lost infant for its mother . . .

The Young One

by Jerome Bixby

As we grow, we learn our roles in life. That isn't always good.

Old Buster was suddenly crouched on stiff legs, right up out of a sound sleep, and his ears were laid back flat against his head, and he was letting out the deep, wet-sounding growl he always used on rattlers.

Young Johnny Stevens looked up in surprise.

The new kid was standing out in the middle of the road, about ten feet away. He'd come up so silently Johnny hadn't even known he was there—until old Buster let out that growl.

Johnny stopped whittling. He sat there on the damp, tree-shaded grass in front of the Stevens farmhouse, his big silver-mounted hunting knife in one hand, the shaved stick in the other, and stared at old Buster.

The dog's head was down, his eyes were up and slitted on the new kid. His lips were curled back tight against his teeth.

The Young One

Johnny started to reach for Buster's scruff, afraid he was getting set to attack. But Buster gave him a mean, panicky, sideways glance, and Johnny pulled back his hand, because he knew his dog. Then Buster whined. His tail went between his legs and he started to walk backward, one slow step after another. He emerged from the shade of the big elm, where he'd been sleeping at Johnny's feet ever since lunch, and kept going backward until he was about twenty feet up the lawn toward the house. Then he stopped and threw back his head as if to howl—but he didn't. He held the pose for a second, his eyes glaring on the new kid down along the sides of his muzzle, and then he turned and ran around the corner of the house.

Buster had never even run from bear. Johnny had once had to drag him off the scent of one.

Johnny turned to look at the new kid, mad clear through and curious as heck at the same time.

The kid looked friendly, curious—and kind of lost. He was dark and thin, with big eyes. His short, stiff, black hair fit his long skull like a cap. His voice had a funny accent, and it was kind of hesitant, almost like he was afraid to talk.

"Hello," he said.

Johnny Stevens stood up. Wood shavings spilled off his lap onto the grass.

"What'd you do to Buster?" he demanded.

"I . . . I don't know. Dogs just don't like me. I'm sorry I frightened him."

Johnny scowled. "You didn't frighten him," he denied formally. "He musta seen something across the road."

"It was me," said the new kid softly.

Johnny turned to look at the corner of the house. Buster was poking his head around, low down, ears still back. The new kid looked over that way too, and Buster ducked out of sight like he was yanked. A second later, Johnny heard the dog's claws gallop across the cellar door along the side of the house and knew Buster must be heading for the field out back, where he went and hid whenever he was punished.

Johnny scowled harder. "Who're you?"

"Kovacs. Hello."

Johnny didn't answer—just stared suspiciously.

"What are you making?" Kovacs asked, after a minute.

"I dunno," Johnny said. Then, because that didn't sound smart, he added, "A cane, maybe. Or a fishing rod. Kovacs what?"

"Bela."

"That's a funny name."

"What is yours?"

"Johnny Stevens."

"Hello, Johnny," Kovacs Bela said again, hopefully.

"Hello," Johnny said sourly.

Kovacs Bela came to the edge of the road, where it gave onto a slope of rock and root-studded dirt that rose a few feet to the Stevens lawn. There he stopped, his thin shadow lying up the slope in front of him, as if he were waiting to be invited.

Johnny sat down again, still scowling. He didn't say anything.

Kovacs half-turned, looking down the road over his shoulder, as if sorry he'd stopped.

They watched a couple of robins chase each other through the sun-bleached rails of the fence across the road. Summer heat danced along the waving tips of wheat in the field beyond, and shimmered up the green-brown sides of the low hillocks that lined the old creek-bed.

Johnny started whittling again.

"You from that new family who bought the old Burman place?" he asked.

"Yes."

"Moved in last week, din'cha? I heard about it."

"Yes."

The robins tired of darting through the fence-rails and set off across the wheatfield, wings blurring, bodies almost brushing the carpet of tips.

"We played around there a lot." Johnny grunted. "The Burman place. Guess we can't now . . . 'cause you moved in."

Kovacs Bela was silent.

"We used the silo for a robber hideout," Johnny said accusingly.

"Silo . . . ?"

"Don't you know what that is?"

Kovacs shook his dark head.

"It's the big round building, like a tin can. You're kinda dumb."

Kovacs bit his lip and stood silently, his big, dark eyes unhappy. "Do you want me to go away?" he asked.

"Sure," said Johnny, still feeling mean.

Kovacs started to turn away, with that aimless look to his movements that means one is going no place in particular—just leaving.

Johnny relented a little. "I was just kiddin' . . . c'mon and sit down."

Kovacs Bela stood for a moment, then smiled hesitantly and came up the dirt slope into the shade of the trees. He sank to the grass and curled his legs under him with an oddly graceful motion. "Thank you," he said.

Johnny peeled a long sliver of bark off the stick with his big, razor-sharp knife. "I wanna know what you did to Buster. How'd you make him act that way?"

"Animals just don't like me."

"Why?"

"My father once said it is the way we sme . . ." Kovacs' voice trailed off. "I don't know. They don't like us."

"Us? You mean your whole family?"

"I—yes."

"You're a funny guy. Where you from, they don't have silos? You talk funny too."

"I am from Hungary."

Johnny looked closely at Kovacs Bela, taking in the dark features, the big eyes, the soft mouth. There was something about the face that disturbed him, but he couldn't pin it down.

"Where's Hungry?" he asked.

"In Europe."

"Oh . . . a foreigner. I guess Buster never saw a foreigner before."

The two robins, or another pair, came hedgehopping back over the wheatfield, arced up over the fence, over the road and into the uppermost branches of the tree directly overhead. They set up a loud chirping, and commenced flitting from branch to branch.

"Where are you from?" Kovacs Bela asked.

"Right here. Michigan." Johnny thought for a second, balancing his big knife on one finger, the heavy blade on one side, the silver-mounted handle on the other. "There's Bela Lugosi in the movies. He's always a monster or something. But Bela's his *first* name."

"It is my first name too. In Hungary, the first name comes last. I should have said my name is Bela Kovacs . . . that is the way you would say it here."

Johnny shook his head, as if wondering at the crazy things foreigners did—and the crazy way they must smell, to wake old Buster up and send him kiting the way he had.

Without being obvious about it, he tried to get a whiff

of Bela Kovacs—but he couldn't smell a thing. Well, dogs could smell lots more than people. Old Buster sure must have.

Bela Kovacs had noticed the headshake. He said a little defensively, "I talk English well, don't I?"

Johnny started to deprecate; but he said instead, honestly, "Yeah. I gotta admit, you talk pretty good."

"We have been in America for almost a year. In New York. And my father taught English to me and my mother before we came."

Johnny was working up considerable interest in his first foreigner. "You mean your father's English?"

"He is Hungarian. He had to teach himself first. It took him a long time. But he said we had to move, and America was the best place for us to go. We brought over some paintings, and my father sold them to buy the farm."

"Your father paints pitchers?"

"My grandfather painted them. He was a famous artist in Hungary."

"What d'you mean, you *had* to move?"

"We . . . we just had to. We had to move to a new country. That's what Father said." Bela Kovacs looked around at the blue summer sky, the heat-shimmering hillocks, the groves of trees that lay along the landscape like clean green cushions, the dusty road that wound through low hills to Harrisville thirty miles to the east. "I am glad we finally moved out here. I did not like New York. In Hungary, we lived in the country."

The Young One

The two robins had been hopping lower and lower in the tree overhead, and now they dropped side by side from the bottom branches to the lawn, where they began searching the thick grass for insects.

One hopped to within a few feet of Bela Kovacs, who still sat with his legs curled under him in that relaxed yet curiously steel-spring position.

Suddenly the robin froze—cocked its head—regarded the boy with a startled beady eye.

Then it chirped a thin note, and both birds streaked away across the lawn as fast as they could go.

Johnny stared after them.

"I like birds," Bela Kovacs said wistfully. "I would not hurt them. I wish they liked me. I wish animals did not hate us."

Johnny began to work up even more interest in his first foreigner—because maybe it wasn't the way he smelled after all.

Because birds could hardly smell anything.

Then he noticed something funny. Bela Kovacs was still looking at the place where the robins had vanished, and Johnny saw what it was that had disturbed him about Bela's face ever since he'd first seen it.

"You have funny eyebrows," he said. "They're awful thick, and they meet in the middle. They grow all the way across."

Bela didn't look at him. The remark seemed to have brought back his shyness. He lowered his head and raised one slender hand to the side of his face, as if wanting to conceal the eyebrows.

After a second, Johnny was sorry he'd said anything.

"Heck, that's okay," he said. "Look—I haven't got any end on this finger." He held up the pinkie he'd caught in the wheel on the well two years ago.

Bela Kovacs stared at the smooth pink end and his straight bar of brows rose at the outsides.

"We're all different," Johnny said—and realized that, curiously, where he had before been teasing this new kid, he was now trying almost to console him. And he wondered, more than ever, what could be wrong with Bela Kovacs to make him act so funny. Guilty, almost—like he was ashamed of something—something he was maybe afraid people would find out.

Bela was sitting in the same position, but somehow he seemed smaller than before, like he was huddled into himself. His hand was still up to his face.

"We're all different," Johnny said again. "My dad always tells me that . . . and he says it doesn't matter. He says for me never to care where anybody comes from, or how funny they look, or anything like that. That's why I don't mind you being a foreigner. I'm sorry Buster acted the way he did."

Bela Kovacs said muffledly, "I'm *so* different."

"Naw."

"I am." Bela looked at Johnny's finger. "I was *born* different."

"Naw," Johnny said again, because he couldn't think of anything else to say. Heck, he knew Bela Kovacs *was* different—anybody could see that. And he was itching to know what the mystery was all about.

He said uncomfortably, "Want to hike or something?"

"Hike?"

"Go walking." Johnny stood up and shoved the hunting knife in his belt. "C'mon, Bela. There's lots of swell places to play—I'll show 'em to you. There's the hollow tree, and the injun fort, and—"

"A real Indian fort?" Bela said, looking up finally, dark eyes wide.

"Naw. We built it outa rocks. And there's the caves, back in the hills . . . miles of 'em. You go in through a little chink that don't look like nothin' at all, and then you flash your light around and there's walls that look like waving cloth, all pink and green and blue, and secret passages and stalatites and stagmites and holes where you can't even see the bottom they're so deep."

"That sounds wonderful," Bela Kovacs said. "Will you take me there, Johnny?"

"Sure. C'mon, I'll pick up my flashlight." Johnny started up the lawn toward the house.

Bela rose gracefully to his feet, as if the steel-spring had suddenly uncoiled, and walked a few steps after Johnny. Then he stopped and looked up at the high summer sun.

"What is the time?" he asked.

"Oh . . . 'bout three o'clock, I guess."

"Is it far—to the caves?"

"Two, three miles."

Bela looked at the grass at his feet. "I have to be home by seven o'clock."

"We can make it easy. C'mon." Johnny started off again.

Bela fell into step. "Johnny—"

"Yeah?"

"I *have* to be home by seven."

"Why?"

"I . . . I just have to. My parents will be terribly angry if I'm not. We will not get lost, or go too far away, will we?"

"Heck, no. I know the caves better'n anybody." Johnny glanced sideways at Bela. "Won't your parents let you play at night? *Mine* do."

"It's—only on certain days that I can't go out at night. Certain times of the month."

"Why?"

"I can't tell you. But I have to be home by seven."

Johnny was intrigued by this new addition to the mystery. "Don't worry," he said. "Nothing'll happen."

They reached the front porch.

"Wait here," said Johnny.

He went into the house and into the kitchen, where Mom was already working on supper, because the Youngs were coming over for bridge tonight, and supper was always something special for guests.

Johnny got his flashlight from under the sink.

Mom looked up from the chicken she was stuffing. "What are you doing, dear?"

"Goin' to the caves."

Mom frowned. "I wish you'd stay away from that place, Johnny. I wish your father would do something to make you. It's so dangerous . . . they go on for miles. Suppose you got lost sometime?"

"I won't get lost," Johnny said contemptuously. "I know every inch."

"Suppose the flashlight failed?"

"Aw, Mom, don't worry . . . I'm just going to show the new kid around."

"The new kid?"

"Bela Kovacs . . . his family bought the old Burman place."

Mom looked surprised and a little pleased. "So they have a little boy! Now you'll have a new playmate. Is he a nice boy?"

Johnny juggled the flashlight. "Well, he's kinda funny. He's a foreigner from Hungry. That's in Europe. I guess he's all right."

"I'd like to meet him."

"He's right outside waitin' . . . c'mon, I'll interduce you."

Johnny started through the house toward the porch where he'd left Bela. Mom smiled and wiped her hands on a towel and followed.

They were just passing through the front room when they heard old Buster barking and snarling like he'd gone crazy.

Buster had Bela Kovacs backed against the porch steps, and was snaking back and forth in front of the boy as if he wanted to attack worse than anything else in the world, but was afraid to.

Bela's dark face had gone bone-colored, and he was half-crouched in an almost animal position, looking ready to move instantly in any direction, including straight up.

Johnny Stevens dropped over the porch-rail and lit beside Bela and shouted, "Buster! Cut it out! *Stop* it!"

Old Buster looked at him with the red-lamp eyes of a mad dog. Watery froth dripped from his stretched lips. His tail was curled so hard between his legs that it pressed up along his belly. He trembled so hard he could hardly stand—but Johnny knew that scared or not, Buster was set to attack any second.

Johnny hissed and clapped his hands in front of him, hard and fast. That meant Buster had better git, or end up with a sore rump.

Buster took a prowling, back-high, head-low step forward. His lips were so curled that his head seemed half teeth.

Mom screamed from the porch, "Johnny, come away!" and Johnny turned his head frantically to look at her, and Buster chose that moment to charge Bela Kovacs.

Then everything happened almost too fast to see.

Johnny felt a tug at his belt, where he'd stuck the hunting

knife, and saw Bela Kovacs swing the heavy blade at Buster's head.

Old Buster lost heart, and turned and ran again, howling his heart out.

Bela Kovacs screamed, *"Silver . . . the knife is silver!"* and he dropped the knife and ran off across the lawn, crying and flapping the hand he'd grabbed the knife-handle with. He turned and ran down the road, faster than Johnny had ever seen a kid run.

Johnny's mother was off the porch and on her knees, frantically examining Johnny to see if he'd been bitten; and Johnny's father drove up just then in the station wagon, craned his neck after Bela Kovacs, and asked what in hell was going on.

After supper, the grown-ups sat around and talked about the new family before starting to play bridge.

Everybody who had met either Mr. or Mrs. Kovacs seemed to like them all right—that was the consensus. Mrs. Young said that McIntyre, the grocer, who was generally looked up to as a pretty good judge of character, had let it be known yesterday that Mr. Kovacs had impressed him favorably, Mr. Kovacs had come in to stock up on food and some implements, and McIntyre had tried to pump him, and Mr. Kovacs had answered the right questions and resisted the rest pleasantly, and McIntyre had liked that.

And Mrs. Kovacs had waited outside the store in the Kovacs' '42 Dodge, and three townsladies said she looked like a nice woman, if a little foreign-looking.

And Junior Murdock, at the gas station, said that the Kovacs Dodge was in very good shape for its age, and showed signs of recent careful overhauling—and Murdoch liked people who cared for their cars, particularly old cars that someone else might lose pride in. He thought it told a lot about them.

Nobody thought them too strange, it seemed—just foreign.

Mrs. Young and Johnny's Mom decided, on the basis of the evidence, to suggest at the next meeting of the Ladies' Club that Mrs. Kovacs be invited to join.

Then the talk got around to what had happened this afternoon.

Old Buster had come back around five o'clock, sneaking out of his hideaway in the field and looking around each time before he put his paw down for a step.

While Mom and Johnny had stayed inside and watched through the front window, and Johnny had blinked back tears of worry, Dad had gone out with his pistol in one hand and coaxed Buster over to him and, with the gun to the animal's head, examined him carefully. Dad knew a lot about animals.

Old Buster wagged his tail and took a couple of laps out of the pan of water Dad carried in his other hand.

Dad came back and said, "He's okay. I don't know what got into him. There are some people animals just hate, and

I guess the Kovacs boy is one of them. It's nothing against him . . . from what Johnny says, he likes animals himself. They just don't like *him.*"

"He tried to kill Buster," Johnny said. He'd been mad about that all afternoon. "He took my knife and tried to kill Buster."

Dad said, "You shouldn't be angry about that, Johnny. It was an instinctive thing to do . . . the kid was probably scared silly. Buster was out for blood, God knows why, and Bela grabbed the knife and took a swipe in self-defense. He's probably sorry he did it."

"I don't care," Johnny said sullenly. "He tried to kill him."

Dad sighed. "It's just lucky that Buster saw the knife and lit out—and that Bela missed with the knife. Bela didn't get bitten, and Buster's all right."

"It wasn't the knife," Johnny said. "Buster ain't scared of my knife. He was scared of *Bela* . . . he ran before he even saw the knife."

"Well," Dad said, "maybe. Anyway, everything's all right now. Nothing really bad happened." He paused. "You know, I feel a little sorry for the kid . . . animals hating him like that. No wonder he acts a little strange. A kid ought to be able to have a pet. Maybe he feels a little inferior to kids who can."

But Johnny was still mad. After Dad finished talking to him, he was less mad than before—but he still resented anyone taking a knife to his dog. No matter what the provocation. And *his* knife to boot.

"I wonder why he dropped the knife and ran," Mom mused. "He yelled that it was silver and acted like it burned his hand."

"Oh," Dad said, "he probably said 'sliver.' Maybe he got a sliver from the knife handle."

Johnny started to object, but let it go. His knife handle was of smooth, worn, hard wood and silver strips—he knew darned well there weren't any slivers on it. But still, he let it go. He'd settle the whole thing in his own way.

When Dad suggested that he go over the next day and apologize to Bela Kovacs for Buster's behavior, and show the new boy that nobody held his actions against him, Johnny said all right.

Because, though he knew Dad was absolutely right and it hadn't been Bela's fault, he still wanted to get back at Bela for trying to kill Buster—and he had a good idea of how to do it.

He'd scare the living daylights out of the kid—and maybe find out what the mysterious reason was why Bela had to be home every night by that time at certain times of the month.

The grownups finally started their bridge game, and Johnny went outside and sat on the porch with Buster and looked up at the big, yellow full moon that rode the night sky like a spotlight.

The Young One

Buster had spent the last two hours prowling around the lawn, smelling everyplace where Bela Kovacs had walked, growling deep in his throat and every so often letting out a scared-sounding howl.

Now Johnny scratched Buster's ears, and thought about tomorrow.

It was a good idea. He'd scare Bela spitless—and then tell him why he'd done it and make friends with him again. Because Bela really wasn't a bad guy . . . he was just a little queer.

The next day Johnny took his flashlight and went over to the old Burman place around three o'clock. He went cross-country instead of down the road, and as he came out of the weed-grown cornfield that old Burman had once tended so lovingly, he saw Bela Kovacs playing in the yard by the windmill.

When Bela saw him, he stood stock-still, dark eyes wide, again with that animal look to him, as if he were ready to run.

Johnny said, "I came over to say I'm sorry Buster tried to bite you."

"Oh." Bela blinked. He had his hands cupped in front of him, about belt-level.

Johnny waited for Bela to say something else, but he didn't. Johnny looked curiously at Bela's cupped hands. "What you got?" he asked.

Bela's mouth twisted. He lifted the top hand, and Johnny

saw that he held a mouse. It was curled into a ball, and its mouth hung wide open—but Johnny noticed it wasn't trying to bite its way loose. Tiny black eyes glittered up in terror.

"I caught it," Bela said. "In the barn."

"What d'you want to catch a *mouse* for?" Johnny said disgustedly. "Why not get a cat?"

Bela blinked again, and Johnny suddenly wondered if Bela hadn't been just about to cry or something, before Johnny showed up, and if he wasn't holding it back now.

"I wanted to make friends with it," Bela said softly. "But it is no different in America. All the animals hate me—fear me."

"Heck, any mouse'd be scared, caught and held that way."

"Not this frightened." Bela knelt and gently placed the mouse on the ground. For a second it stayed there, a huddled gray ball—then legs erupted and it bounded off so fast that halfway to the barn it tripped and rolled over twice, and when it reached a gap between two boards in the side of the barn, it bounced off hard because of bad aim. Then it vanished, hind legs scrabbling.

"See?" said Bela. "It runs in terror. So would a cat. I have never had a pet." He straightened and gave Johnny his shy, lonely smile. "I am sorry about yesterday too, Johnny. I am sorry I tried to hurt your dog. I did not mean—"

"Aw," Johnny said uncomfortably, remembering how Dad had felt sorry for Bela last night—and remembering what he planned to do today in the caves. "Aw . . . forget it."

Bela took Johnny into the farmhouse to meet his parents.

Mr. Kovacs was a big, handsome, middle-aged man who moved the same smooth way Bela did. And Mrs. Kovacs moved that way too—Johnny noticed it the instant he came through the front door into the living room, for Bela's parents had just been finishing their lunch, and when they saw Johnny come in, they rose from the table with Old World courtesy. And with that strange animal grace.

"Father and Mother," said Bela, "this is Johnny Stevens, the boy I met yesterday."

Mr. Kovacs took Johnny's hand and shook it firmly and gently—and Johnny could tell, from the size of Mr. Kovacs' hand and the hard feel of its palm against his own, that Mr. Kovacs was very, very strong.

And a funny thing—when Johnny took his hand away, the ends of his fingers rubbed against something sort of bristly in Mr. Kovacs' hard palm. It felt almost like Dad's cheek, just after he shaved—like short whisker stubble.

But that was silly. Nobody had hair on their palms. He'd probably just felt dried skin peeling away from work calluses . . .

Mrs. Kovacs, a slim, pretty woman, nodded pleasantly and said, with an accent much more pronounced than Bela's, "How do you do, Mr. Stevens."

Johnny swelled a little. It was the first time anyone had ever called him Mr. Stevens.

"I'm pleased to meet you," he said.

"Bela has told us what happened yesterday," Mr. Kovacs said. "Please, may we add our apologies to his? It is unfortunate—but animals just do not like us. It is a peculiarity of our family."

"Heck," Johnny said. "*I* came over to apologize. And to play with Bela."

Mrs. Kovacs smiled and said almost exactly what Johnny's mother had said the day before: "How nice . . . for Bela to have such a nice boy his own age to play with."

It was Johnny's turn to smile shyly. He looked away and for the first time got a look at the inside of the Kovacs home.

The last time he'd been in this house, about three weeks ago, it had been bare walls and refuse-cluttered floors. Now there was furniture—mostly ordinary stuff. But there were some things—the round table in the middle of the room, for instance, and that big bookcase-desk against the wall— that were pretty foreign-looking. And the pictures—most of them were in fancier, heavier frames than any he'd ever seen, and a lot of them were of funny foreign buildings. And the tablecloth, and the candlesticks and lamps and the rug—oh, lots of the smaller things around the room had a foreign look. A sort of solid, warm, old look.

Mr. Kovacs, noting Johnny's interest, said in a deep bass voice. "We brought many of our things from Hungary."

"It looks nice," Johnny said.

"Thank you," said Mr. Kovacs gravely.

Mrs. Kovacs commenced to clear the table, and Johnny glanced casually at the plates . . . and when he saw what the lunch had consisted of, his jaw sagged, and he looked again.

Raw meat. A roast of beef, it looked like—except it wasn't roasted. And nothing else. A big platter of red, blood-juicy beef in the middle of the table, three red-stained plates at the chair-places, glasses, and a pitcher of water.

Again Mr. Kovacs noted Johnny's interest. Or his amazement.

"Raw meat," he said, a little heavily, "is good for the blood. We eat raw beefsteak once or twice a week, young man."

"Oh," said Johnny, trying not to stare so hard. "I guess I read about that someplace myself—'bout raw meat being good for you. But I don't think . . ." His voice trailed off.

"You do not think you would like it," Mrs. Kovacs smiled, picking up the plates. "But you are too polite to say so."

Johnny nodded uncomfortably.

"Now," said Mr. Kovacs, "come here, young man."

Johnny moved to stand before the man's chair. He didn't know exactly why—except that he felt somehow that Mr. Kovacs was a friendly man.

Mr. Kovacs looked appreciatively—almost critically—at Johnny's well-muscled arms and firm neck and clear eyes.

"You are in good health," he said.

"I . . . I guess so."

"You will make a good playmate for our Bela," Mr. Kovacs said. "He is very active. Do you know the country here?"

"I've lived here all my life."

"Good. You will tell Bela of any dangers that exist, yes?"

"Sure."

"Good. Now, Bela, why don't you show your new friend around the house?"

Mrs. Kovacs began to remove the platter of raw beef. Mr. Kovacs reached out and took one of the remaining chunks and bit into it with teeth that, when he opened his mouth wide, were startlingly long and white and, from the way the meat tore, sharp.

He chewed and looked at Johnny again, a little reflectively. Johnny and Bela were over by the bookcase by the stairs. Bela was showing Johnny what Hungarian writing looked like.

Mrs. Kovacs looked too, and her large eyes—now they were almost luminous—traveled up and down Johnny's body, along the muscular arms and legs, dwelt on the tanned throat. She licked her lips.

"In the old country . . ." she sighed in Hungarian.

"Eva," said Mr. Kovacs, softly but warningly, also in Hungarian.

"Ah, *imadot* Ferenc, I am only thinking. But *look* at him . . ."

The Young One

Mr. Kovacs smiled at the expression on her face. "Sh-h, now, Eva. We have left all that behind . . . it is best not even to think."

"*Sajnos* . . ." Mrs. Kovacs picked up a small piece of beef and bit into it with teeth as long and sharp as her husband's. She sighed again. "A new country, a new life . . . I know, my dear."

"You are unhappy, Eva?"

"Unhappy?" Eva Kovacs smiled down at him, and since her lower lip concealed the points of her teeth, it was quite a pleasant smile. "Only my belly suffers. I am happy that we are safe, Ferenc."

He took her hand and pressed it against his shoulder. "The old country, the old life . . . it is impossible to live that way any longer, Eva. We are known. Not you, perhaps, nor I, nor little Bela, but *we* . . . all of us . . . known by signs familiar to the smallest child. While here—here they do not know us, or even believe in us—and we must let it remain so. We must forsake the old ways."

"You are not disappointed in America, then."

He shook his massive head. "America is best, in every way. There is no tradition to expose us. The political situation is good. And living conditions, and opportunity. No, mamma, I am well content here—except—" he put his big hands palms up on the table before him and flexed them and then slowly made fists around the clean-shaven stubble on the palms—"except at this time of the month, when the moon turns her full face to us . . ."

"Yes," said Eva Kovacs softly. "Yes."

"But beef does not taste so bad my dear. Not so bad, at least, as a silver bullet."

Mrs. Kovacs popped the last of the beef into her mouth, chewed powerfully, and swallowed. She seemed to be tasting it in her throat, feeling it, almost analyzing it as it went toward her stomach. "No," she said slowly. "Once you are used to it, it is not bad. But—"

"Do not think about it, Eva."

"We cannot even chase the cow," she said softly. "We must go and buy—"

"I know."

Mrs. Kovacs looked across the room again at Johnny Stevens, and her large eyes grew larger.

"Eva," Mr. Kovacs said, a little sharply. "You would not think of—"

"No, no," she said, and licked blood from fingers which seemed to have grown just a little hairier, and the nails a little longer. "Of course not, *imadot* Ferenc. It is just when I remember . . ."

"We must forget."

"And they are so *healthy* here . . ."

"We must never *change* again, Eva. Never."

"And Bela?"

Ferenc Kovacs sighed. "He is too young yet—too young to know. We must be sure that he is always with us when he *changes*. Soon he will be old enough to control the *change*, as we do—then we must worry no longer in our new home."

The Young One

Bela had been showing Johnny his room, which held an old posterbed, a very old maple bureau, and a carved chest full of fascinating toys such as Johnny had never seen before.

Now the boys came back to the living room, and Bela said, "Mother, we are going out to play."

"All right, Bela. But remember—come home before seven o'clock."

"Yes, mamma."

"You know what time of the month this is, don't you?"

"Yes, mamma." Bela looked uncomfortably at Johnny. "I will be back."

"You *must,*" said Mr. Kovacs. "Just as you did in New York. You know why, Bela . . ." He turned to Johnny. "You will not keep our Bela out late, will you? You see— he is not well . . . that is why it is very important that he return home before nightfall."

"Oh," said Johnny. "I'll be careful. I mean, I'll . . . I won't . . ." And he looked away in confusion, thinking of what he planned to do in the cave.

Mr. Kovacs' big eyes were still on his face when he looked up, and Johnny felt they were looking right through his own eyes at the inside of his skull.

"I think," said Mr. Kovacs, "that you had better be."

Bela's parents came to the door and stood in the sunshine, and as Johnny and Bela turned to wave at them from the edge of the cornfield, Johnny noticed for the first time that their eyebrows were just like Bela's—straight, thick bars of hair that ran right across their foreheads.

The entrance to the caves was just a black chink in the rocks on the hillside. They climbed up toward it, leaping from one big boulder to the next under the afternoon sun.

They reached the black hole, and felt the coolness of it on their faces, even in the sunshine.

Bela hung back when Johnny started to go right in.

"Johnny . . ." he said.

"Yeah?"

"Don't forget . . . I *have* to be back before seven."

Johnny put his hands on his hips. "Well, f'gosh sakes, yes! I heard it enough. What's so awful that'll happen to you if you don't? D'you have to take medicine or something?"

Bela shook his head. "I can't tell you. But . . . you won't get lost or anything, will you?"

"No," said Johnny emphatically, crossing his fingers behind his back.

"You heard what my parents said . . . I have to be home before the moon rises."

"The *moon!* What's the moon got to do with it?"

Bela just looked nervously at the black hole in the hillside.

And Johnny didn't ask about it again. He just sniffed. "The moon, f'gosh sakes!" as if he were dismissing it as something else crazy that foreigners—especially Hungarians—worried about. Because he knew he had a better way of finding out.

"Johnny . . . perhaps I had better not go in. Not now."

Johnny put a jeer in his voice. "Scared?"

"Not for the reasons you think," Bela said, dark eyes flashing. "You do not understand."

"Well, come on, then . . . I promise—" the crossed fingers again—"I won't get lost."

Johnny started again into the black chink. Bela hesitated for a second, and then followed.

Actually, Johnny thought, as they made their way through the narrow fissure into increasing darkness, the crossed fingers weren't necessary—because he wasn't planning to really get lost; only to *pretend* to get lost.

And he wasn't sure he was going to do even that, now— not if Bela was *sick*. That was different. Maybe it explained a lot—even old Buster's behavior. Dogs sometimes got funny around sick people.

But he wasn't sure that that *was* the explanation. It sounded a little fishy to him. Why all the mystery, if Bela was just sick? Or was it some awful-to-*gosh* disease? If so, why was Bela let out to play and maybe give the disease to someone else? And Mr. Kovacs had said that Bela was very active. That didn't sound like he was sick. And Bela sure didn't look sick.

Johnny decided he'd wait and decide what to do later.

The floor of the chink dipped down and turned at a right angle, and they were inside the caves.

Johnny turned on his flashlight. And heard Bela gasp.

All around them were curtains and draperies and carpets and fountains of stone—gray, pink, blue, green, lavender, stretching from where they stood to a sharp sixty-foot down-slope ahead of them, which led to the cave floor below and off into inky shadows that looked almost like solids.

Johnny played the beam of light around, giving Bela a good look at everything worth seeing here near the entrance. Then he said, "Let's start down."

They made their way across ripples of pastel-shaded stone to where the down-slope began. The sounds they made started to echo, and the air was very dry and cool.

The beam of the flashlight was hard and bright, and the blackness pressed in on it as if trying to squash it down to pencil-thinness—but the beam moved like lightning, cutting like a knife, and wherever it opened the blackness it revealed wonders of color and shape.

"The waves in the slope make steps," Johnny said, pointing the light downward. "See? We can go down that way. How do you like it?"

"It is beautiful," Bela whispered.

They started down, Johnny keeping the light always on their footing and guiding their progress down the face of rock by familiar rippling formations and splashes of color.

At last they reached the bottom, and Johnny said, "This way."

As they started across the uneven floor of the cave, Bela asked, "Do you know the time, Johnny?"

" 'Bout four . . . you got lotsa time."

And soon the caves became so beautiful that Bela forgot entirely to worry about the time.

The Young One

They passed fountains and sprays and mists and museums of stone, gleaming with colors purer and more delicate than any ever seen on Earth's surface. They passed marching stalagmites of green and blue and bright orange, here and there united with drooping stalactites to form arching passageways and gardens of pillars. They moved slowly beneath walls of rippled stone, as if blue or pink or purple lava had been frozen in midflow.

They passed lakes of blue-black water, so still and smooth that one had almost to touch them to be convinced that they weren't glass.

They moved up vast slopes of colored stone, like insects up a giant Christmas tree ornament, and when they reached the top, Johnny would select this dark passage or that and lead them on into royal chambers of purple and white, and then up a curving crimson staircase to a balcony of coral, pink and green, where more passages offered further mysteries to be explored.

They moved along the edges of crevices so deep that a penny dropped made no sound—not even the whisper of an echo.

Once Johnny turned off his light and told Bela to stand still, and they listened to the silence which cannot be qualified, the silence which is absolute—the silence that exists only underground.

They heard their own hearts beating.

At last Johnny was sure the time must be about six o'clock.

"We'd better get started back," he told Bela. "If you're

going to get home by seven. This way."

And he led the way back to the place where they had entered the caves. And there he pretended to get lost.

It was easy. Bela was new to the caves. He probably wouldn't recognize the entrance even if Johnny flashed his light up the long slope right to the chink where they'd come in.

Johnny wasn't sure yet whether he wanted to keep up the pretense for more than a few minutes—maybe he'd just throw a short scare into Bela, and then take him on out of the caves so he could go home by seven. After all, if Bela was sick . . .

But he wasn't sure about that. It still sounded fishy. And he was more curious than ever to know what the mystery was all about—even if it *was* some kind of disease.

He said worriedly, "Bela . . . I . . . I'm not sure which way we go from here. I think maybe I'm lost . . ."

And he looked to see what effect it would have on the Hungarian boy.

Bela's eyes grew huge. "Oh, *no* . . . Johnny, you do not mean it! You *promised!*"

Johnny pretended to be confused—even afraid. "I . . . I'm sorry," he stammered. "I just lost the way. I was so interested showing you around. Gosh, Bela—"

"But, Johnny, I *have* to get out. I have to get home before . . ."

"Come on," Johnny said, making his voice worried. "Maybe . . . maybe it's this way."

And he led Bela in a huge circle through the pillars and passages and hanging stone curtains that surrounded the entrance. It took about half an hour, and then they were right back where they'd started from—within a hundred feet of the entrance.

Johnny said, "I just don't know where we *are!*"

"What time do you think it is?" Bela asked, his voice terrified.

"Six-thirty, about."

Bela shuddered and looked at Johnny, his eyes shining enormously in the light. "Johnny, I have to get *out* . . ."

Johnny put panic in his voice. "Well, what can *I* do? I'm sorry! I'm scared too! Maybe we'll *never* get out!"

"Try," Bela begged. "Try, Johnny . . . can't you remember the way?"

Looking at Bela in the light, at the big dark eyes and smooth brown skin and white straight teeth and lithe body, Johnny decided abruptly that the story about Bela's being sick must be phony. It was something *else*—there was some other reason why Bela was so frantic about being home by seven, and why his parents were so emphatic on the same point. Some real strange, funny reason—and Johnny wanted to know what.

He decided to do as he'd originally planned—keep Bela down here and watch to see what happened.

He turned around as if in indecision. "I think . . . I think maybe it's off this way. Come on!"

And he led Bela in a circle the other way around, by a

slightly different route, and they ended up by the entrance again.

Johnny knew it must be nearly seven by now. He kept a sharp eye on Bela while pretending to search for the entrance chink that was really right up the slope over their heads.

Would Bela know, somehow, when seven o'clock had arrived? And was it something that would happen to him right at seven that he was afraid of? But how could he know the time? . . . and what could happen down here in the caves? Or was it something his parents would do to him later, as punishment for not getting home by that time?

"Johnny!" Bela said suddenly, close by Johnny in the blackness, a quaver in his voice.

Johnny stopped his pretense of searching, and put the beam of light on Bela. "Yeah?"

Bela was trembling all over, and he was looking up at the roof of the cave. As Johnny watched, he hunched his shoulders a little—sort of cringed—and his face got even tighter, as if he saw something horrible coming at him right down through the blackness, the solid rock.

"It is almost seven . . . Johnny . . . *do something . . .* it is going to *happen!*"

"What's going to happen? *What* can I do?"

"I do not know," Bela cried, and echoes came back, *I do not know, do not know . . .*

"You don't know what I can do?"

"I do not know . . ." . . . *do notknow, notknow, know, know* . . .

"You don't know what's going to happen?"

"I do not know! I am frightened . . . it never happened to me away from home before . . . Johnny, you *promised* . . . ah, mamma, mamma, *mamma*—" and Bela began to cry. He sank to a heap on the colored stone floor, and tears rolled down his cheeks and splashed on the stone and made the colors deeper, and he wailed things in Hungarian until he could hardly talk any more but just cried.

"You don't know what's going to happen?" Johnny asked, amazed.

Bela choked trying to talk, and coughed hard, and the echoes came back like footsteps across his frantic voice. "Yes, I know—but I do not know what it is, or why, it just *happens* . . . ah, mamma, *mamma* . . ."

Suddenly his back stiffened, and his hands clawed out in front of him. His streaming eyes rolled up to Johnny's face. He whined like an animal. "Johnny . . . it is seven . . . the moon is rising . . . I can feel it . . ."

"*Feel* the moon? Down *here*? How can—"

"It does not matter where . . . I can *feel* it . . . I can feel . . . mamma, mamma—ah, ah, *ah!*"

And Bela's face twisted into an expression of such terror and agony that Johnny was suddenly chilled—and he decided that his joke had gone far enough. In fact, all of a sudden he was pretty darned scared—he hadn't expected anything like this! Golly, if Bela really *was* sick . . .

He bent over the huddled figure on the cave floor and pointed his flashlight upward.

"Bela, look!" he said loudly. "Look up there . . . *there's* where we came in! Come on—let's go out!"

Bela didn't answer.

"Bela . . . *c'mon.*"

Bela moved, and his fingernails scratched the rock so hard it sounded like they'd tear off.

Johnny began to tremble. He looked down, the flashlight still pointing up.

Bela's eyes gleamed up at him from the floor—enormous, yellowish in the reflected light, glassy, fixed—somehow baleful.

As Johnny watched, they seemed to move closer together and get yellower.

Johnny was so startled he dropped the flashlight. It thumped on the stone at his feet, and glass broke and the light went out.

In the blackness—the utter thick blackness—Johnny heard a scuffling sound near his feet, and a low, soft, animal snarl.

He yelled and leaped back. His foot struck the flashlight, and even as he went down he got one hand on it, and with the other hand he dragged his big hunting knife out of his belt. He hit hard on his side. He pressed the flashlight button and prayed that it would work.

It did.

Bela was gone.

Wide-eyed, Johnny rolled over. Kneeling there, he darted the light this way and that. Finally he found his voice.

"B-Bela . . ." he quavered.

Nothing happened.

He got to his feet and stood shaking. "Bela?"

There was a claws-on-stone sound from the blackness behind him.

He whirled, his neck stiff and cold, and lashed the beam of light across the shadows. He held his hunting knife hard, the point straight out, ready to stab or slice from almost any angle.

At first he saw nothing. Rocks. Curtains and pillars of colored stone. Black shadows that seemed to lean toward him.

Then a low shadow moved at the corner of his vision.

He swung the light that way.

Two yellow eyes, low against the stone floor, blazed back at him.

"B-Bela?" Johnny whispered, and lifted the light so that it shone directly on the possessor of the eyes.

The creature slitted the eyes and snarled to reveal sharp white fangs and charged.

Mr. and Mrs. Kovacs were looking both furious and terrified at the same time. They stood by the big table in the living room, where they'd been sitting playing some kind of game with big colored cards, when Johnny came bursting in to tell them what had happened in the caves.

"I'm sorry," Johnny said, for the dozenth time—and wiped a hand across his tear-stained cheeks.

"I didn't mean to do it . . . it was just a joke. Please, call Sheriff Morris and ask him to get a posse out . . . they'll find Bela, honest they will!"

Mr. Kovacs' large eyes were brilliant with anger—and his deep voice was almost a snarl. "*I* will go look for Bela, young man—and you had better go home. I do not think we want to see you any more!"

Johnny turned miserably toward the door.

There was a growl from the darkness right outside.

Mrs. Kovacs gasped, "*Bela* . . ."

The creature came panting through the open door and made a beeline for Johnny's leg.

Johnny said, "It isn't Bela . . . it's that darned wolf cub!"

He dodged and dropped to one knee and cuffed the cub playfully on the side of the head.

It snarled like a lapdog and backed off and put its belly against the floor. Its tiny ears were flat against its head, just as old Buster's had been when he'd first seen Bela, and its yellow eyes gleamed hungrily on Johnny's throat.

It charged again, stubby legs pumping.

Johnny caught it neatly by the scruff of the neck and shook it gently. It snapped and snarled and waved its legs.

"I'll be darned," he said, forgetting for the moment that Mr. Kovacs had practically ordered him out of the house. "The little feller must've followed me here . . ."

"You saw the little wolf tonight?" Mr. Kovacs said

sharply, eyes widening and glowing a little brighter.

"Sure. In the cave. Just after Bela ran off. It tried to bite me then too, and now it followed me all the way to your place." Johnny grinned feebly, looking from Mr. Kovacs' rather grim face to Mrs. Kovacs' somehow relieved one. "I guess it wants to eat me or something."

"I suppose," said Mr. Kovacs heavily, "it does."

"I'll take it outside and turn it loose again," Johnny said.

"Again?"

The cub swung from Johnny's grasp, rolling its yellow eyes hungrily at the nearest finger. Johnny nodded. "I carried it up out of the caves, after I gave up hollering for Bela. Figured it wasn't right to let it die down there. Maybe when it gets older, I'll shoot it if I see it . . . but now I figured to give it a chance, it's so young."

"Oh, give him to me, young man," said Mrs. Kovacs. "He's so cute!" And she took the wolf cub from Johnny's arms before Johnny could protest it was dangerous, and cuddled it in her own. It whined and looked up at her with its big yellow eyes, and didn't struggle at all to free itself.

Johnny was too unhappy to wonder at that, though, or even notice it.

"Now go home, young man," said Mr. Kovacs.

Johnny turned to the door again. "Will you turn it loose afterwards, Mr. Kovacs? You won't kill it, will you?"

"I will not kill it."

"And you better call the sheriff to help you look for Bela.

I'll help too, if . . . if you want. I know the caves like—"

"Bela will be all right," Mr. Kovacs said.

"When you find him, will you please tell him I'm sorry for what I did?"

"Yes."

Johnny had reached the front door when Mrs. Kovacs said something soft in Hungarian, and Mr. Kovacs grunted and said, "Young man."

Johnny turned. "Yes, sir?"

The wolf cub was on the table, and Mr. Kovacs was thoughtfully scratching the scruff of its neck.

"Young man," Mr. Kovacs said slowly. "I do not want to be harsh. I have thought it over. What you did was not very nice—but I think it is understandable. I think it may be forgiven. And you came to us immediately and told us about it—and now you have offered to help undo what you have done."

"Yes, sir?"

"You may come here as often as you wish, and play with our Bela."

Johnny brightened. "Yes, sir! Thank you!"

"Provided you never do anything like that again."

"Yes, sir. I mean, no, sir!"

"Now," said Mr. Kovacs a little intently. "I would like to make absolutely certain of what happened in the cave. It happened like this, yes? Our Bela became sick; you dropped your flashlight; when you turned the light on again, Bela was gone."

"That's right, sir."

"You did *not* see where Bela went."

"No, sir."

"And then you saw the little wolf."

"Uh, huh." Johnny grinned. "It was a dope to wander in there. Lucky I came along."

"M'm," said Mr. Kovacs. "Yes." His eyes, which had become a little larger as he questioned Johnny, lost some of their wary glow; and his fingers, which had become just a tiny bit hairier, relaxed. "Now, you had better go. I will . . . find Bela. Good night, young man."

"Good night, Mr. Kovacs. Good night, Mrs. Kovacs."

As Johnny turned to leave again, Mr. Kovacs said, "Another thing, young man."

Johnny paused.

"I was not entirely truthful with you. Our Bela is not really sick. It is just that at certain times of the month, he is expected to be home before nightfall because . . . well, I believe you might call it a custom. A Hungarian custom. An old family custom. It must be observed. Do you understand?"

"Yes, sir."

"We will not tell Bela what you did . . . if you will promise never to tell anyone what happened tonight."

"Yes, sir."

"We would not want to be thought queer by our neighbors. After all, young man, customs differ. We are all of us different."

"Yes, sir. My father taught me that."

"Did he teach you to keep promises?"

Johnny grinned. "He licks me when I don't."

"Do you promise, then?"

"Yes."

"You will make a good playmate for our Bela, as I said. Good night, young man."

Smiling, Johnny Stevens left. When he reached the edge of the cornfield, he began to whistle at the full moon overhead. He wondered if the moon always rose at seven in Hungary . . .

Naw. Maybe it was just a time set so Bela would always be home before it happened, and observe whatever the custom was. But, heck, lots of times the moon rose earlier than seven. Even the full moon, like tonight—it always rose when the sun set. Four o'clock sometimes, in winter.

Maybe—Johnny nodded, remembering something from school—maybe the Kovacs figured the time for Bela to be home by the seasons, by the months. Even by the—the— latitudes.

What a funny custom. Maybe someday Bela would tell him about it . . .

Mr. Kovacs looked thoughtfully at his son.

"We could have lost all," he told his wife, "but for a boy dropping a flashlight. Our new country is good to us. Now—the time has come when we must tell Bela what he is."

Optical Illusion

by Mack Reynolds

In acquiring followers, it is not always wise to depend upon blind faith.

Molly brought my plate, silver, and side dishes and placed them before me without fuss or comment. I was an old customer, and one of the things I liked about Molly was that she never fussed over me.

I usually make a practice of eating after the rush hour, but today I was early and the restaurant crowded. It was only a matter of time before someone would want to share my table.

I didn't look up when he asked, "Is this seat taken?" His voice was high, almost to the point of shrillness, in spite of his attempt to control it.

"No," I told him, "go right ahead."

He hung his cane, or umbrella, whatever it was, over the back of his chair and fumbled his hat underneath it before climbing to his seat. Then he picked up the menu from where it stood between the catsup and napkins.

"Nothing fit to eat," he muttered finally.

I said, "The pot pie is quite good today."

Molly came up and he said to her, "I'll have the swiss steak, miss. Green peas, french fries. I'll decide on the dessert later."

"Coffee?"

"Milk."

I don't know what it was that first gave me the idea that the person seated across the table from me wasn't a midget at all. Not a midget or dwarf, but a child pretending adulthood and doing a fantastically good job of it. As I say, I don't know what it was that gave me the hint, possibly I'm more susceptible to such intuitiveness than the next man.

But whatever it was, he knew almost as soon as I did.

That is, he knew that I'd caught on to him, and somehow it frightened me. The whole idea was so bizarre—a child, not yet in his teens, passing himself off, for some reason of his own, as a mature, if stunted, adult.

"So," he said, his shrill voice almost a hiss. He put down his fork. "So . . ."

How can I describe that cold voice? The voice of a child . . . but not a child. Not a child as we know one.

I reached for the sugar, which was there where it always is at the end of the table next to the salt and pepper and the mustard jar. I measured out a spoonful very carefully without looking up at him. As I have said, somehow I was afraid.

He said, still softly, "So at last a stupid human has penetrated my disguise."

Optical Illusion

A *human,* he had said.

His voice was a child's, but his words dug into me viciously. "Ah, so that surprises you, my curious friend. You wonder, eh?" There was a sneering quality now, a contemptuous overtone.

I cleared my throat, tried to cover my confusion by taking a gulp of the coffee. "I don't know what you mean . . . sir."

He chuckled and mimicked, "I don't know what you mean . . . sir." Then his voice snapped over at me, even as he kept his tone low. "Why did you hesitate before adding the *sir,* eh? Why?" He didn't wait for an answer. "I'll tell you why. Because somehow you've discovered that my age is less than I would have it known."

He was boiling with rage, and in spite of his size and the public nature of our whereabouts, I was afraid of him. Why, I didn't know. Somehow I sensed that—impossibly— he could destroy me at will.

I fumbled my cup back into its saucer, kept my face averted.

"You're terrified," he snapped again. "You recognize your master even as you wonder about him."

"My master?" I said. Who did he think . . .

"Your master," he repeated. "Mankind's master. The new race. The super-race, *Homo Superior,* if you will. He is here, my snooping friend, and you, you and your stupid nation-divided, race-divided, class-divided, religion-divided humanity will never stand before him."

It was hard for me to assimilate. I had come into my

157

favorite restaurant for my midday meal. It had been a routine day, and I had expected it to continue as one. Now, I had been startled so many times in the past few minutes that I felt I was in a state of shock.

"Oh, it's been suggested before," he went on, seemingly welcoming this opportunity to explain to me, to gloat over me. "The possibility that mutations would develop, a super-race, a super-humanity as far above man as man is above the ape."

"How . . . what . . ."

He cut me off. "What difference if it was the atomic bomb, laboratory experiments, or only nature's continual plodding advance? The fact remains, we are here, a considerable number of us, and in a few years, when we have developed our full capacities, man will hear from us. Ah, how he will hear!"

Long ago an icy hand had gripped my heart. Now it squeezed.

"Why," I stumbled. "Why tell me all this? Surely you wouldn't disguise yourself if you didn't wish to keep it all a secret."

He laughed mockingly. There was still much of the immature in him, super-race or nay.

"Because it doesn't make any difference," he whispered. "None at all. Ten minutes from now, you will remember nothing of this conversation. Hypnotism, my stupid *Homo sapiens,* can be a developed art when practiced on the lower orders."

His voice went hard and incisive. "Look up into my eyes," he ordered.

I had no power to resist. Slowly my face came up. I could *feel* his eyes drill into mine.

"This you will forget," he ordered. "All of this conversation, all of this experience, you will forget."

He came to his feet, took his time about securing his things, and then left.

Molly came over later. "Gee," she said, "that little midget that was just here, he sure tips good."

"I would imagine," I told her. I was still shaken. "He probably has a substantial source of income."

"Oh," Molly said, making conversation as she cleaned up. "You been talking to him?"

"Yes," I told her, "we had quite a discussion." I added thoughtfully, "And as a result I have duties to perform."

I came to my own feet and reached up for my hat and cane, where they hung on their usual hook.

I thought: *possibly man has more of a chance than these hidden enemies realize. Mental powers beyond us they may have, although they would seem lacking in the more kindly qualities. But this one hadn't been as sharp as he liked to think himself. Hypnotic powers he might possess beyond our understanding, but that didn't prevent him from making a very foolish error. He hadn't caught on to the fact that I'm blind.*

Idiot's Crusade

by Clifford D. Simak

Is he good or is he bad? Read his story and decide.

For a long time I was the village idiot, but not any longer—although they call me "dummy" still and even worse than that.

I'm a genius now, but I won't let them know.

Not ever.

If they found out, they'd be on their guard against me.

No one has suspected me and no one will. My shuffle is the same and my gaze as vacant and my mumblings just as vague as they ever were. At times, it has been hard to remember to keep the shuffle and the gaze and mumblings as they were before, times when it was hard not to overdo them. But it's important not to arouse suspicion.

It all started the morning I went fishing.

I told Ma I was going fishing while we were eating breakfast, and she didn't object. She knows I like fishing. When I fish, I don't get into trouble.

"All right, Jim," she said. "Some fish will taste real good."

"I know where to get them," I told her. "That hole in the creek just past Alf Adams' place."

"Now don't you get into any fracas with Alf," Ma warned me. "Just because you don't like him—"

"He was mean to me. He worked me harder than he should have. And he cheated me out of my pay. And he laughs at me."

I shouldn't have said that, because it hurts Ma when I say someone laughs at me.

"You mustn't pay attention to what people do," said Ma, speaking kind and gentle. "Remember what Preacher Martin said last Sunday. He said—"

"I know what he said, but I still don't like being laughed at. People shouldn't laugh at me."

"No," Ma agreed, looking sad. "They shouldn't."

I went on eating my breakfast, thinking that Preacher Martin was a great one to be talking about humility and patience, knowing the kind of man he was, and how he was carrying on with Jennie Smith, the organist. He was a great one to talk about anything at all.

After breakfast, I went out to the woodshed to get my fishing tackle, and Bounce came across the street to help me. After Ma, Bounce is the best friend I have. He can't talk to me, of course—not actually, that is—but neither does he laugh at me.

I talked to him while I was digging worms and asked

him if he wanted to go fishing with me. I could see he did, so I went across the street to tell Mrs. Lawson that Bounce was going along. He belonged to her, but he spent most of his time with me.

We started out, me carrying my cane pole and all my fishing stuff, and Bounce walking at my heels, as if I were someone he was proud to be seen walking with.

We went past the bank, where Banker Patton was sitting in the big front window, working at his desk and looking like the most important man in all of Mapleton, which he was. I went by slow so I could hate him good.

Ma and me wouldn't be living in the old tumbledown house we're living in if Banker Patton hadn't foreclosed on our home after Pa died.

We went out past Alf Adams' place, which is the first farm out of town, and I hated him some, too, but not as hard as Banker Patton. All Alf had done was work me harder than he should have, then cheat me of my pay.

Alf was a big, blustery man and a good enough farmer, I guess—at least he made it pay. He had a big new barn, and it's just like him not to paint it red, the way any proper barn is painted, but white with red trim. Who ever heard of paint trim on a barn?

Just beyond Alf's place, Bounce and I turned off the road and went down across the pasture, heading for the big hole in the creek.

Alf's prize Hereford bull was way off in another corner

of the pasture with the rest of the stock. When he saw us, he started coming for us, not mean or belligerent, but just investigating and ready for a fight if one was offered him. I wasn't afraid of him, because I'd made friends with him that summer I had worked for Alf. I used to pet him and scratch behind his ears. Alf said I was a crazy fool and someday the bull would kill me.

"You can never trust a bull," Alf said.

When the bull was near enough to see who it was, he knew we meant no harm, so he went back across the pasture again.

We got to the hole and I started fishing, while Bounce went up the stream to do some investigating. I caught a few fish, but they weren't very big and they weren't biting very often and I got disinterested. I like to fish, but to keep my interest up, I have to catch some.

So I got to daydreaming. I began wondering if you marked off a certain area of ground—a hundred feet square, say— and went over it real careful, how many different kinds of plants you'd find. I looked over a patch of ground next to where I was sitting, and I could see just ordinary pasture grass and some dandelions and some dock and a couple of violets and a buttercup which didn't have any flowers as yet.

Suddenly, when I was looking at the dandelion, I realized I could see *all* that dandelion, not just the part that showed above the ground!

* * *

I don't know how long I'd been seeing it that way before realizing it. And I'm not certain that "seeing" is the right word. Maybe "know" would be better. I *knew* how that dandelion's big taproot went down into the ground and how the little feathery roots grew out of it, and I knew where all the roots were, how they were taking water and chemicals out of the ground, how reserve food was stored in the root and how the dandelion used the sunlight to convert its food into a form it could use. And the funniest thing about it was that I had never known any of it before.

I looked at the other plants, and I could see all of them the same way. I wondered if something had gone wrong with my eyes and if I would have to go around looking into things instead of at them, so I tried to make the new seeing go away and it did.

Then I tried to see the dandelion root again and I saw it, just the way I had before.

I sat there, wondering why I had never been able to see that way before and why I was able to now. And while I was wondering, I looked into the pool and tried to see down into the pool and I could, just as plain as day. I could see clear to the bottom of it and into all the corners of it, and there were lunkers lying in there, bigger than any fish that ever had been taken from the creek.

I saw that my bait was nowhere near any of the fish, so I moved it over until it was just in front of the nose of one of the biggest ones. But the fish didn't seem to see it, or if he did, he wasn't hungry, for he just lay there, fanning the water with his fins and making his gills work.

I moved the bait down until it bumped his nose, but he still didn't pay any attention to it.

So I made the fish hungry.

Don't ask me how I did it. I can't tell you. I all at once knew I could and just how to do it. So I made him hungry and he went for that bait like Bounce grabbing a bone.

He pulled the cork clear under, and I heaved on the pole and hoisted him out. I took him off the hook and put him on the stringer, along with the four or five little ones I'd caught.

Then I picked out another big fish and lowered my bait down to him and made him hungry.

In the next hour and a half, I just about cleaned out all the big fish. There were some little ones left, but I didn't bother with them. I had the stringer almost full, and I couldn't carry it in my hand, for then the fish would have dragged along the ground. I had to sling it over my shoulder, and those fish felt awfully wet.

I called Bounce and we went back to town.

Everyone I met stopped and had a look at my fish and wanted to know where I'd got them and what I'd caught them on and if there were any left or had I taken them all. When I told them I'd taken all there was, they laughed fit to kill.

I was just turning off Main Street, on my way home, when Banker Patton stepped out of the barbershop. He smelled nice from the bottles of stuff that Jake, the barber, uses on his customers.

He saw me with my fish and stopped in front of me. He looked at me and looked at the fish, and he rubbed his fat hands together. Then he said, like he was talking to a child, "Why, Jimmy, where did you get all those fish?" He sounded a little bit, too, like I might not have a right to them and probably had used some low-down trick to get them.

"Out in the hole on Alf's place," I told him.

All at once, without even trying to do it, I saw him the same way I had seen the dandelion—his stomach and intestines and something that must have been his liver—and up above them all, surrounded by a doughy mass of pink, a pulsating thing that I knew must be his heart.

I guess that's the first time anybody ever *really* hated someone else's guts.

I shot out my hands—well, not my hands, for one was clutching the cane pole and the other was busy with the fish—but it felt almost exactly as if I'd put them out and grabbed his heart and squeezed it hard.

He gasped once, then sighed and wilted, like all the starch had gone out of him, and I had to jump out of the way so he wouldn't bump into me when he fell.

He never moved after he hit the ground.

Jake came running out of his barbershop.

"What happened to him?" he asked me.

"He just fell over," I said.

Jake looked at him. "It's a heart attack. I'd know it anywhere. I'll run for Doc."

He took off up the street for Doc Mason while other people came hurrying out of the places along the street.

There was Ben from the cheese factory and Mike from the pool hall and a couple of farmers who were in the general store.

I got out of there and went on home, and Ma was pleased with the fish.

"They'll taste real good," she said, looking at them. "How did you come to catch that many, Jim?"

"They were biting good," I said.

"Well, you hurry up and clean them. We'll have to eat some right away, and I'll take some over to Preacher Martin's, and I'll rub salt in the others and put them in the cellar where it's good and cool. They'll keep for several days."

Just then, Mrs. Lawson ran across the street and told Ma about Banker Patton.

"He was talking to Jim when it happened," she told Ma.

Ma said to me, "Why didn't you tell me, Jim?"

"I never got around to it," I said. "I was showing you these fish."

So the two of them went on talking about Banker Patton, and I went out to the woodshed and cleaned the fish. Bounce sat alongside me and watched me do it, and I swear he was as happy over those fish as I was, just like he might have had a hand in catching them.

Now I don't want you to think I'm trying to make you believe Bounce actually talked, because he didn't. But it was just as if he'd said those very words.

"It was a nice day, Bounce," I said, and Bounce said he'd thought so, too. He recalled running up and down the stream and how he'd chased a frog and the good smell there was when he stuck his nose down to the ground and sniffed.

People all the time are laughing at me and making cracks about me and trying to bait me because I'm the village idiot, but there are times when the village idiot has it over all of them. They would have been scared they were going crazy if a dog talked to them, but I didn't think it was strange at all. I just thought how much nicer it was now that Bounce could talk and how I wouldn't have to guess at what he wanted to say. I never thought it was queer at all, because I always figured Bounce could talk if he only tried, being a smart dog.

So Bounce and I sat there and talked while I cleaned the fish. When I came out of the woodshed, Mrs. Lawson had gone home, and Ma was in the kitchen, getting a skillet ready to cook some of the fish.

"Jim, you . . ." she hesitated, then went on, "Jim, you didn't have anything to do with what happened to Banker

Patton, did you? You didn't push him or hit him or anything?"

"I never even touched him," I said, and that was true. I certainly hadn't touched him.

In the afternoon, I went out and worked in the garden. Ma does some housework now and then, and that brings in some money, but we couldn't get along if it wasn't for the garden. I used to work some, but since the fight I had with Alf over him not paying me, she don't let me work for anyone. She says if I take care of the garden and catch some fish, I'm helping out enough.

Working in the garden, I found a different use for my new way of seeing. There were worms in the cabbages, and I could see every one of them, and I killed them all by squeezing them, the way I'd squeezed Banker Patton. I found a cloudy sort of stuff on some of the tomato plants and I suppose it was some kind of virus, because it was so small I could hardly see it at first. So I magnified it and could see it fine, and I made it go away. I didn't squeeze it like I did the worms. I just made it go away.

It was fun working in the garden, when you could look down into the ground and see how the parsnips and radishes were coming and could kill the cutworms you found there and know just how the soil was and if everything was all right.

We'd had fish for lunch and we had fish again for supper, and after supper, I went for a walk.

Before I knew it, I was walking by Banker Patton's place and, going past, I felt the grief inside the house.

I stood out on the sidewalk and let the grief come into me. I suppose that outside any house in town, I could have felt just as easily whatever was going on inside, but I hadn't known I could and I hadn't tried. It was only because the grief in the Patton house was so deep and strong that I noticed it.

The banker's oldest daughter was upstairs in her room, and I could feel her crying. The other daughter was sitting with her mother in the living room and neither of them was crying, but they seemed lost and lonely. There were other people in the house, but they weren't very sad. Some neighbors, probably, who'd come in to keep the family company.

I felt sorry for the three of them, and I wanted to help them. Not that I'd done anything wrong in killing Banker Patton, but I felt sorry for those women, because, after all, it wasn't their fault the way Banker Patton was, so I stood there, wishing I could help them.

And all at once I felt that perhaps I could, and I tried first with the daughter who was upstairs in her room. I reached out to her, and I told her happy thoughts. It wasn't easy to start with, but pretty soon I got the hang of it, and it wasn't hard to make her happy. Then I made the other two happy and went on my way, feeling better about what I'd done to the family.

I listened in on the houses I passed. Most of them were happy, or at least contented, though I found a couple that were sad. Automatically, I reached out my mind and gave them happiness. It wasn't that I felt I should do something good for any particular person. To tell the truth, I don't remember which houses I made happy. I just thought if I was able to do a thing like that, I should do it. It wasn't right for someone to have that kind of power and refuse to use it.

Ma was sitting up for me when I got home. She was looking kind of worried, the way she always does when I disappear for a long time and she don't know where I am.

I went up to my room and got into bed and lay awake for a long time, wondering how come I could do all the things I could and how, suddenly, today I was able to do them when I'd never been able to before. But finally I went to sleep.

The situation is not ideal, of course, but a good deal better than I had any reason to expect. It is not likely that one should find on every alien planet, a host so made to order for our purpose as is this one of mine.

It has accepted me without recognizing me, has made no attempt to deny itself to me or to reject me. It is of an order of intelligence which has enabled it, quickly and efficiently, to make use of those most-readily manipulated of my abilities, and this has aided me greatly in my observations. It is fairly mobile and consorts freely with its kind, which are other distinct advantages.

I reckon myself fortunate, indeed, to have found so satisfactory a host so soon upon arrival.

When I got up and had breakfast, I went outside and found Bounce waiting for me. He said he wanted to go and chase some rabbits, and I agreed to go along. He said since we could talk now, we ought to make a good team. I could stand up on a stump or a pile of rocks or even climb a tree, so I could overlook the ground and see the rabbit and yell out to him which way it was going, and he could intercept it.

We went up the road toward Alf's place, but turned off down across the pasture, heading for some cutover land on the hill across the creek.

When we were off the road, I turned around to give Alf a good hating, and while I was standing there, hating him, a thought came into my mind. I didn't know if I could do it, but it seemed to be a good idea, so I tried.

I moved my seeing up to Alf's barn and went right through and came out in the middle of the haymow, with hay packed all around me. But all the time, you understand, I was standing out there in the pasture with Bounce, on our way to chase some rabbits.

I'd like to explain what I did next and how I did it,

but mostly what worries me is how I knew enough to do it—I mean enough about chemical reaction and stuff like that. I did something to the hay and something to the oxygen, and I started a fire up there in the center of the haymow. When I saw it was started good, I got out of there and was in myself again, and Bounce and I went on across the creek and up the hill.

I kept looking back over my shoulder, wondering if the fire might not have gone out, but all at once there was a little trickle of smoke coming out of the haymow, opening up under the gable's end.

We'd got up into the cutover land by that time, and I sat down on a stump and enjoyed myself. The fire had a good start before it busted out and there wasn't a thing that could be done to save the barn. It went up with a roar and made the prettiest column of smoke you've ever seen.

On the way home, I stopped at the general store. Alf was there and he seemed much too happy to have just lost his barn.

But it wasn't long until I understood why he was so happy.

"I had her insured," he told Bert Jones, the storekeeper, "plumb up to the hilt. Anyhow, it was too big a barn, a lot bigger than I needed. When I built it, I figured I was going to go into milking heavier than I've done and would need the space."

Bert chuckled. "Handy fire for you, Alf."

"Best thing that ever happened to me. I can build another barn and have some cash left over."

I was pretty sore about bungling it, but I thought of a way to get even.

After lunch, I went up the road again and out into Alf's pasture and hunted up the bull. He was glad to see me, although he did a little pawing and some bellowing just to show off.

I had wondered all the way out if I could talk to the bull the way I talked to Bounce and I was afraid that maybe I couldn't, for Bounce was bound to be smarter than a bull.

I was right, of course. It was awful hard to make that bull understand anything.

I made the mistake of scratching behind his ears while I tried to talk to him, and he almost went to sleep. I could feel just how good the scratching felt to him. So I hauled off and kicked him in the ribs to wake him up, so he would pay attention. He did pay a little closer attention and even did a little answering, but not much. A bull is awful dumb.

But I felt fairly sure I'd got my idea across, for he started acting sore and feisty, and I'm afraid that I overdid it just a mite. I made it to the fence ahead of him and went over without even touching it. The bull stopped at the fence and stood there, pawing and raising Cain, and I got out of there as fast as I could go.

I went home fairly pleased with myself for thinking up

as smart a thing as that. I wasn't surprised in the least to hear that evening that Alf had been killed by his bull.

It wasn't a pretty way to die, of course, but Alf had it coming to him, the way he beat me out of my summer wages.

I was sitting in the pool hall when the news was brought in by someone, and they all talked about it. Some said Alf had always claimed you couldn't trust no bull, and someone else said he'd often said I was the only one who'd ever gotten along with this particular bull, and he was scared all the time I was there for fear the bull would kill me.

They saw me sitting there and they asked me about it and I acted dumb and all of them laughed at me, but I didn't mind their laughing. I knew something they didn't know. Imagine how surprised they'd be if they ever learned the truth!

They won't, of course.

I'm too smart for that.

When I went home, I got a tablet and a pencil and started to write down the names of all my enemies—everyone who had ever laughed at me or done mean things to me or said mean things about me.

The list was pretty long. It included almost everyone in town.

I sat there thinking and I decided maybe I shouldn't kill everyone in town. Not that I couldn't, for I could have, just as slick as anything. But thinking about Alf and Banker

Patton, I could see there wasn't any lasting satisfaction in killing people you hate. And I could see as plain as day that if you killed a lot of people, it could leave you pretty lonesome.

I read down through the list of names I'd made, and I gave a couple of them the benefit of a doubt and scratched them out. I read those that were left over, and I had to admit that every one of them was bad. I decided that if I didn't kill them, I'd have to do something else about them, for I couldn't let them go on being bad.

I thought about it a long time, and I remembered some of the things I'd heard Preacher Martin say, although, as I've mentioned before, he's a great one to be saying them. I decided I'd have to lay aside my hate and return good for evil.

I am puzzled and disturbed, although that, perhaps, is the normal reaction when one attaches oneself to an alien being. This is a treacherous and unprincipled species and, as such, an incalculably important one to study.

I am continually amazed at the facility with which my host has acquired the use of my talents, continually appalled by the use he makes of them. I am more than puzzled by his own conviction that he is less intelligent than his fellows; his actions during my acquaintance with him do not bear this out. I wonder if it may not be a racial trait, a sort of cult-attitude of inferiority, that it may be ill-mannered to think of oneself in any other way.

Idiot's Crusade

But I half suspect that he may have sensed me in some way without my knowing it and may be employing this strange concept as a device to force me from his mind. Under such a circumstance, it would not be prime ethics for me to remain with him—but he has proved to be such an excellent seat of observation that I am loath to leave him.

The fact is, I don't know. I could, of course, seize control of his mind and thus learn the truth of this and other matters which are perplexing me. But I fear that, in doing so, I would destroy his effectiveness as a free agent and thus impair his observational value. I have decided to wait before taking such a drastic measure.

I ate breakast in a hurry, being anxious to get started. Ma asked me what I was going to do and I said just walk around a bit.

First off, I went to the parsonage and sat down outside the hedge between it and the church. Pretty soon, Preacher Martin came out and began to walk up and down in what he called his garden, pretending he was sunk in holy thought, although I always suspected it was just an act to impress old ladies who might see him.

I put out my mind real easy and finally I got it locked with his so neatly, it seemed that it was me, not him, who was walking up and down. It was a queer feeling, I can tell you, for all the time I knew good and well that I was sitting there back of the hedge.

He wasn't thinking any holy thoughts at all. He was going

over in his mind all the arguments he intended to use to hit up the church board for a raise in salary. He was doing some minor cussing out of some of the members of the board for being tightfisted skinflints and that I agreed with, because they surely were.

Taking it easy, just sort of stealing in on his thoughts, I made him think about Jennie Smith, the organist, and the way he was carrying on with her, and I made him ashamed of himself for doing it.

He tried to push me away, though he didn't know it was me; he just thought it was his own mind bringing up the matter. But I wouldn't let him push the thought away. I piled it on real heavy.

I made him think how the people in the church trusted him and looked to him for spiritual leadership, and I made him remember back to when he was a younger man, just out of seminary, and looked on his lifetime work as a great crusade. I made him think of how he'd betrayed all the things he'd believed in then, and I got him down so low, he was almost bawling. Then I made him tell himself that owning up was the only way he could absolve himself. Once he'd done that, he could start life over again and be a credit to himself and his church.

I went away, figuring I'd done a fair job of work on him, but knowing that I'd have to check up on him every now and then.

At the general store, I sat around and watched Bert Jones

sweep out the place. While he was talking to me, I sneaked into his mind and recalled to him all the times he'd paid way less than market prices for the eggs the farmers brought in, and the habit of sneaking in extra items on the bills he sent out to his charge customers, and how he'd cheated on his income tax. I scared him plenty on the income tax, and I kept working at him until he'd about decided to make it right with everyone he'd cheated.

I didn't finish the job airtight, but I knew I could come back any time I wanted to, and in a little while, I'd make an honest man of Bert.

Over at the barbershop, I watched Jake cut a head of hair. I wasn't too interested in the man Jake was working on—he lived four or five miles out of town—and at the moment, I figured that I'd better confine my work to the people in the village.

Before I left, I had Jake plenty worried about the gambling he'd been doing in the back room at the pool hall and had him almost ready to make a clean breast of it to his wife.

I went over to the pool hall. Mike was sitting back of the counter with his hat on, reading the baseball scores in the morning paper. I got a day-old paper and pretended to read it. Mike laughed and asked me when I'd learned to read, so I laid it on good and thick.

When I left, I knew, just as soon as I was out the door, he'd go down into the basement and dump all the moonshine down the drain, and before too long, I'd get him to close up the back room.

Over at the cheese factory, I didn't have much chance to work on Ben. The farmers were bringing in their milk and he was too busy for me to really get into his mind. But I did manage to make him think of what would happen if Jake ever caught him with Jake's wife. And I knew when I could catch him alone, I could do a top-notch job on him, for I saw he scared easy.

And that's the way it went.

It was tough work, and at times I felt it was just too much of a job. But then I'd sit down and remind myself that it was my duty to keep on—that for some reason this power had been given me, and that it was up to me to use it for all it was worth. And furthermore, I was not to use it for myself, for any selfish ends, but for the good of other people.

I don't think I missed a person in the village.

Remember how we wondered if there might not be unseen flaws in this plan of ours? We went over it most carefully and could find none, yet all of us feared that some might show up in actual practice. Now I can report there is one. It is this:

Accurate, impersonal observation is impossible, for as soon as one introduces one's self into a host, his abilities become available to the host and at once become a factor which upsets the norm.

Idiot's Crusade

As a result of this, I am getting a distorted picture of the culture of this planet. Reluctant to intervene before, I am now convinced that I must move to take command of the situation.

Bert, now that he's turned honest, is the happiest man you ever saw. Even losing all the customers who got sore at him when he explained why he paid them back some money, doesn't bother him. I don't know how Ben is getting along—he disappeared right after Jake took the shotgun to him. But, then, everyone agrees Ben was overdoing it when he went to Jake and told him he was sorry for what had been going on. Jake's wife is gone, too, and some folks say she followed Ben.

To tell the truth, I am well satisfied with the way everything's turned out. Everyone is honest, and no one is fooling around with anyone else, and there ain't a lick of gambling or drinking going on in town. Mapleton probably is the most moral village in the United States.

I feel that perhaps it turned out the way it did because I started out by conquering my own evil thoughts and, instead of killing all the folks I hated, set out to do them good.

I'm a little puzzled when I walk through the streets at night, because I don't pick up near as many happy thoughts as I used to. In fact, there are times when it keeps me busy almost all night long, getting them cheered up. You'd think honest folks would be happy folks. I imagine it's because, now they're good instead of bad, they're not so given to giddy pleasures, but are more concerned with the solid, worthwhile side of life.

I'm a little worried about myself. While I did a lot of good, I may have done it for a selfish reason. I did it, perhaps partly, to make up for killing Alf and Banker Patton. And I did it not for just people, but for people I know. That doesn't seem right. Why should only people I know benefit?

Help! Can you hear me? I'm trapped! I can neither control my host nor can I escape from him. Do not under any circumstances let anyone else try to use another member of this race as a host!

Help!

Can you hear me?

Help!

I've sat up all night, thinking, and now the way is clear.

Having reached my decision, I feel important and humble, both at once. I know I'm a chosen instrument for good and must not let anything stop me. I know the village was no more than a proving ground, a place for me to learn what I could really do. Knowing now, I'm determined to use the power to its utmost for the good of all humanity.

Ma's been saving up a little money for a long time for a decent burial.

I know just where she hides it.

It's all she's got.

But it's enough to get me to the U.N.

One for the Road

by Stephen King

Here's why Downeasters don't like kissing.

It was quarter past ten and Herb Tooklander was thinking
of closing for the night when the man in the fancy overcoat
and the white, staring face burst into Tookey's Bar, which
lies in the northern part of Falmouth. It was the tenth of
January, just about the time most folks are learning to live
comfortably with all the New Year's resolutions they broke,
and there was one hell of a northeaster blowing outside.
Six inches had come down before dark and it had been
going hard and heavy since then. Twice we had seen Billy
Larribee go by high in the cab of the town plow, and the
second time Tookey ran him out a beer—an act of pure
charity my mother would have called it, and my God knows
she put down enough of Tookey's beer in her time. Billy
told him they were keeping ahead of it on the main road,
but the side ones were closed and apt to stay that way
until next morning. The radio in Portland was forecasting

another foot and a forty-mile-an-hour wind to pile up the drifts.

There was just Tookey and me in the bar, listening to the wind howl around the eaves and watching it dance the fire around on the hearth. "Have one for the road, Booth," Tookey says, "I'm gonna shut her down."

He poured me one and himself one and that's when the door cracked open and this stranger staggered in, snow up to his shoulders and in his hair, like he had rolled around in confectioner's sugar. The wind billowed a sand-fine sheet of snow in after him.

"Close the door!" Tookey roars at him. "Was you born in a barn?"

I've never seen a man who looked that scared. He was like a horse that's spent an afternoon eating fire nettles. His eyes rolled toward Tookey and he said, "My wife— my daughter—" and he collapsed on the floor in a dead faint.

"Holy Joe," Tookey says. "Close the door, Booth, would you?"

I went and shut it, and pushing it against the wind was something of a chore. Tookey was down on one knee holding the fellow's head up and patting his cheeks. I got over to him and saw right off that it was nasty. His face was fiery red, but there were gray blotches here and there, and when you've lived through winters in Maine since the time Woodrow Wilson was President, as I have, you know those gray blotches mean frostbite.

"Fainted," Tookey said. "Get the brandy off the back bar, will you?"

I got it and came back. Tookey had opened the fellow's coat. He had come around a little; his eyes were half open and he was muttering something too low to catch.

"Pour a capful," Tookey says.

"Just a cap?" I asks him.

"That stuff's dynamite," Tookey says. "No sense overloading his carb."

I poured out a capful and looked at Tookey. He nodded. "Straight down the hatch."

I poured it down. It was a remarkable thing to watch. The man trembled all over and began to cough. His face got redder. His eyelids, which had been at half-mast, flew up like window shades. I was a bit alarmed, but Tookey only sat him up like a big baby and clapped him on the back.

The man started to retch, and Tookey clapped him again.

"Hold on to it," he says, "that brandy comes dear."

The man coughed some more, but it was diminishing now. I got my first good look at him. City fellow, all right, and from somewhere south of Boston, at a guess. He was wearing kid gloves, expensive but thin. There were probably some more of those grayish-white patches on his hands, and he would be lucky not to lose a finger or two. His coat was fancy, all right; a three-hundred-dollar job if ever I'd seen one. He was wearing tiny little boots that hardly came up over his ankles, and I began to wonder about his toes.

"Better," he said.

"All right," Tookey said. "Can you come over to the fire?"

"My wife and my daughter," he said. "They're out there. . . in the storm."

"From the way you came in, I didn't figure they were at home watching the TV," Tookey said. "You can tell us by the fire as easy as here on the floor. Hook on, Booth."

He got to his feet, but a little groan came out of him and his mouth twisted down in pain. I wondered about his toes again, and I wondered why God felt he had to make fools from New York City who would try driving around in southern Maine at the height of a northeast blizzard. And I wondered if his wife and his little girl were dressed any warmer than him.

We hiked him across to the fireplace and got him sat down in a rocker that used to be Missus Tookey's favorite until she passed on in '74. It was Missus Tookey that was responsible for most of the place, which had been written up in *Down East* and the *Sunday Telegram* and even once in the Sunday supplement of the Boston *Globe*. It's really more of a public house than a bar, with its big wooden floor, pegged together rather than nailed, the maple bar, the old barn-raftered ceiling, and the monstrous big fieldstone hearth. Missus Tookey started to get some ideas in her head after the *Down East* article came out, wanted to start calling the place Tookey's Inn or Tookey's Rest, and I admit it has sort of a Colonial ring to it, but I prefer plain old Tookey's Bar. It's one thing to get uppish in the summer, when the state's full of tourists, another thing altogether in the winter, when you and your neighbors have to trade together. And there had been plenty of winter nights, like this one, that Tookey and I had spent all alone together, drinking scotch and water or just a few beers. My own Victoria passed on in '73, and Tookey's was a place to go where there were enough voices to mute the steady ticking of the deathwatch beetle—even if there was just Tookey and me, it was enough. I wouldn't have felt the same about it if the place had been Tookey's Rest. It's crazy but it's true.

We got this fellow in front of the fire and he got the shakes harder than ever. He hugged onto his knees and his teeth clattered together and a few drops of clear mucus spilled off the end of his nose. I think he was starting to realize that another fifteen minutes out there might have been enough to kill him. It's not the snow, it's the wind-chill factor. It steals your heat.

"Where did you go off the road?" Tookey asked him.

"S-six miles s-s-south of h-here," he said.

Tookey and I stared at each other, and all of a sudden I felt cold. Cold all over.

187

"You sure?" Tookey demanded. "You came six miles through the snow?"

He nodded. "I checked the odometer when we came through t-town. I was following directions . . . going to see my wife's s-sister . . . in Cumberland . . . never been there before . . . we're from New Jersey . . ."

New Jersey. If there's anyone more purely foolish than a New Yorker it's a fellow from New Jersey.

"Six miles, you're sure?" Tookey demanded.

"Pretty sure, yeah. I found the turnoff but it was drifted in . . . it was . . ."

Tookey grabbed him. In the shifting glow of the fire his face looked pale and strained, older than his sixty-six years by ten. "You made a right turn?"

"Right turn, yeah. My wife—"

"Did you see a sign?"

"Sign?" He looked up at Tookey blankly and wiped the end of his nose. "Of course I did. It was on my instructions. Take Jointer Avenue through Jerusalem's Lot to the 295 entrance ramp." He looked from Tookey to me and back to Tookey again. Outside, the wind whistled and howled and moaned through the eaves. "Wasn't that right, mister?"

"The Lot," Tookey said, almost too soft to hear. "Oh my God."

"What's wrong?" the man said. His voice was rising. "Wasn't that right? I mean, the road looked drifted in, but I thought . . . if there's a town there, the plows will be out and . . . and then I . . ."

He just sort of trailed off.

"Booth," Tookey said to me, low. "Get on the phone. Call the sheriff."

"Sure," this fool from New Jersey says, "that's right. What's wrong with you guys, anyway? You look like you saw a ghost."

Tookey said, "No ghosts in the Lot, mister. Did you tell them to stay in the car?"

"Sure I did," he said, sounding injured. "I'm not crazy."

Well, you couldn't have proved it by me.

"What's your name?" I asked him. "For the sheriff."

"Lumley," he says. "Gerard Lumley."

He started in with Tookey again, and I went across to the telephone. I picked it up and heard nothing but dead silence. I hit the cutoff buttons a couple of times. Still nothing.

I came back. Tookey had poured Gerard Lumley another tot of brandy, and this one was going down him a lot smoother.

"Was he out?" Tookey asked.

"Phone's dead."

"Hot damn," Tookey says, and we look at each other. Outside the wind gusted up, throwing snow against the windows.

Lumley looked from Tookey to me and back again.

"Well, haven't either of you got a car?" he asked. The anxiety was back in his voice. "They've got to run the engine to run the heater. I only had about a quarter of a tank of gas, and it took me an hour and a half to . . . Look, will you *answer* me?" He stood up and grabbed Tookey's shirt.

"Mister," Tookey says, "I think your hand just ran away from your brains, there."

Lumley looked at his hand, at Tookey, then dropped it. "Maine," he hissed. He made it sound like a dirty word about somebody's mother. "All right," he said. "Where's the nearest gas station? They must have a tow truck—"

"Nearest gas station is in Falmouth Center," I said. "That's three miles down the road from here."

"Thanks," he said, a bit sarcastic, and headed for the door, buttoning his coat.

"Won't be open, though," I added.

He turned back slowly and looked at us.

"What are you talking about, old man?"

"He's trying to tell you that the station in the Center belongs to Billy Larribee and Billy's out driving the plow, you damn fool," Tookey says patiently. "Now why don't you come back here and sit down, before you bust a gut?"

He came back, looking dazed and frightened. "Are you telling me you can't . . . that there isn't . . . ?"

"I ain't telling you nothing," Tookey says. "You're doing all the telling, and if you stopped for a minute, we could think this over."

"What's this town, Jerusalem's Lot?" he asked. "Why was the road drifted in? And no lights on anywhere?"

I said, "Jerusalem's Lot burned out two years back."

"And they never rebuilt?" He looked like he didn't believe it.

"It appears that way," I said, and looked at Tookey. "What are we going to do about this?"

"Can't leave them out there," he said.

I got closer to him. Lumley had wandered away to look out the window into the snowy night.

"What if they've been got at?" I asked.

"That may be," he said. "But we don't know it for sure. I've got my Bible on the shelf. You still wear your Pope's medal?"

I pulled the crucifix out of my shirt and showed him. I was born and raised Congregational, but most folks who live around the Lot wear something—crucifix, St. Christopher's medal, rosary, something. Because two years ago, in the span of one dark October month, the Lot went bad. Sometimes, late at night, when there were just a few regulars drawn up around Tookey's fire, people would talk it over. Talk around it is more like the truth. You see, people in the Lot started to disappear. First a few, then a few more, then a whole slew. The schools closed. The town stood empty for most of a year. Oh, a few people moved in—mostly damn fools from out of state like this fine specimen here— drawn by the low property values, I suppose. But they didn't last. A lot of them moved out a month or two after they'd moved in. The others . . . well, they disappeared. Then the town burned flat. It was at the end of a long dry fall.

They figure it started up by the Marsten House on the hill that overlooked Jointner Avenue, but no one knows how it started, not to this day. It burned out of control for three days. After that, for a time, things were better. And then they started again.

I only heard the word "vampires" mentioned once. A crazy pulp truck driver named Richie Messina from over Freeport way was in Tookey's that night, pretty well liquored up. "Jesus Christ," this stampeder roars, standing up about nine feet tall in his wool pants and his plaid shirt and his leather-topped boots. "Are you all so damn afraid to say it out? Vampires! That's what you're all thinking, ain't it? Jesus-jumped-up-Christ in a chariot-driven sidecar! Just like a bunch of kids scared of the movies! You know what there is down there in 'Salem's Lot? Want me to tell you? Want me to tell you?"

"Do tell, Richie," Tookey says. It had got real quiet in the bar. You could hear the fire popping, and outside the soft drift of November rain coming down in the dark. "You got the floor."

"What you got over there is your basic wild dog pack," Richie Messina tells us. "That's what you got. That and a lot of old women who love a good spook story. Why, for eighty bucks I'd go up there and spend the night in what's left of that haunted house you're all so worried about. Well, what about it? Anyone want to put it up?"

But nobody would. Richie was a loudmouth and a mean drunk and no one was going to shed any tears at his wake, but none of us were willing to see him go into 'Salem's Lot after dark.

"Be screwed to the bunch of you," Richie says. "I got my four-ten in the trunk of my Chevy, and that'll stop anything in Falmouth, Cumberland, *or* Jerusalem's Lot. And that's where I'm goin'."

He slammed out of the bar and no one said a word for a while. Then Lamont Henry says, real quiet, "That's the last time anyone's gonna see Richie Messina. Holy God." And Lamont, raised to be a Methodist from his mother's knee, crossed himself.

"He'll sober off and change his mind," Tookey said, but he sounded uneasy. "He'll be back by closin' time, makin' out it was all a joke."

But Lamont had the right of that one, because no one ever saw Richie again. His wife told the state cops she thought he'd gone to Florida to beat a collection agency, but you could see the truth of the thing in her eyes—sick, scared eyes. Not long after, she moved away to Rhode Island. Maybe she thought Richie was going to come after her some dark night. And I'm not the man to say he might not have done.

Now Tookey was looking at me and I was looking at Tookey as I stuffed my crucifix back into my shirt. I never felt so old or so scared in my life.

Tookey said again, "We can't just leave them out there, Booth."

"Yeah. I know."

We looked at each other for a moment longer, and then he reached out and gripped my shoulder. "You're a good man, Booth." That was enough to buck me up some. It seems like when you pass seventy, people start forgetting that you are a man, or that you ever were.

Tookey walked over to Lumley and said, "I've got a four-wheel-drive Scout. I'll get it out."

"For God's sake, man, why didn't you say so before?" He had whirled around from the window and was staring angrily at Tookey. "Why'd you have to spend ten minutes beating around the bush?"

Tookey said, very softly, "Mister, you shut your jaw. And if you get the urge to open it, you remember who made that turn onto an unplowed road in the middle of a goddamned blizzard."

He started to say something, and then shut his mouth. Thick color had risen up in his cheeks. Tookey went out to get his Scout out of the garage. I felt around under the bar for his chrome flask and filled it full of brandy. Figured we might need it before this night was over.

Maine blizzard—ever been out in one?

The snow comes flying so thick and fine that it looks like sand and sounds like that, beating on the sides of your car or pickup. You don't want to use your high beams because they reflect off the snow and you can't see ten feet in front of you. With the low beams on, you can see maybe fifteen feet. But I can live with the snow. It's the wind I don't like, when it picks up and begins to howl, driving the snow into a hundred weird flying shapes and sounding like all the hate and pain and fear in the world. There's death in the throat of a snowstorm wind, white death— and maybe something beyond death. That's no sound to hear when you're tucked up all cozy in your own bed with the shutters bolted and the doors locked. It's that much worse if you're driving. And we were driving smack into 'Salem's Lot.

"Hurry up a little, can't you?" Lumley asked.

I said, "For a man who came in half frozen, you're in one hell of a hurry to end up walking again."

He gave me a resentful, baffled look and didn't say anything else. We were moving up the highway at a steady twenty-five miles an hour. It was hard to believe that Billy Larribee had just plowed this stretch an hour ago; another two inches had covered it, and it was drifting in. The strongest gusts of wind rocked the Scout on her springs. The headlights showed a swirling white nothing up ahead of us. We hadn't met a single car.

About ten minutes later Lumley gasps: "Hey! What's that?"

He was pointing out my side of the car; I'd been looking dead ahead. I turned, but was a shade too late. I thought I could see some sort of slumped form fading back from the car, back into the snow, but that could have been imagination.

"What was it? A deer?" I asked.

"I guess so," he says, sounding shaky. "But its eyes—they looked red." He looked at me. "Is that how a deer's eyes look at night?" He sounded almost as if he were pleading.

"They can look like anything," I says, thinking that might be true, but I've seen a lot of deer at night from a lot of cars, and never saw any set of eyes reflect back red.

Tookey didn't say anything.

About fifteen minutes later, we came to a place where the snowbank on the right of the road wasn't so high because the plows are supposed to raise their blades a little when they go through an intersection.

"This looks like where we turned," Lumley said, not sounding too sure about it. "I don't see the sign—"

"This is it," Tookey answered. He didn't sound like himself at all. "You can just see the top of the signpost."

"Oh. Sure." Lumley sounded relieved. "Listen, Mr. Tooklander, I'm sorry about being so short back there. I was cold and worried and calling myself two hundred kinds of fool. And I want to thank you both—"

"Don't thank Booth and me until we've got them in this car," Tookey said. He put the Scout in four-wheel drive and slammed his way through the snowbank and onto Jointner Avenue, which goes through the Lot and out to 295. Snow flew up from the mudguards. The rear end tried to break a little bit, but Tookey's been driving through snow since Hector was a pup. He jockeyed it a bit, talked to it, and on we went. The headlights picked out the bare indication of other tire tracks from time to time, the ones made by Lumley's car, and then they would disappear again. Lumley was leaning forward, looking for his car. And all at once Tookey said, "Mr. Lumley."

"What?" He looked around at Tookey.

"People around these parts are kind of superstitious about 'Salem's Lot," Tookey says, sounding easy enough—but I could see the deep lines of strain around his mouth, and the way his eyes kept moving from side to side. "If your people are in the car, why, that's fine. We'll pack them up, go back to my place, and tomorrow, when the storm's over, Billy will be glad to yank your car out of the snowbank. But if they're not in the car—"

"Not in the car?" Lumley broke in sharply. "Why wouldn't they be in the car?"

"If they're not in the car," Tookey goes on, not answering, "we're going to turn around and drive back to Falmouth Center and whistle for the sheriff. Makes no sense to go wallowing around at night in a snowstorm anyway, does it?"

"They'll be in the car. Where else would they be?"

I said, "One other thing, Mr. Lumley. If we should see anybody, we're not going to talk to them. Not even if they talk to us. You understand that?"

Very slow, Lumley says, "Just what are these superstitions?"

Before I could say anything—God alone knows what I

would have said—Tookey broke in. "We're there."

We were coming up on the back end of a big Mercedes. The whole hood of the thing was buried in a snowdrift, and another drift had socked in the whole left side of the car. But the taillights were on and we could see exhaust drifting out of the tailpipe.

"They didn't run out of gas, anyway," Lumley said.

Tookey pulled up and pulled on the Scout's emergency brake. "You remember what Booth told you, Lumley."

"Sure, sure." But he wasn't thinking of anything but his wife and daughter. I don't see how anybody could blame him, either.

"Ready, Booth?" Tookey asked me. His eyes held on mine, grim and gray in the dashboard lights.

"I guess I am," I said.

We all got out and the wind grabbed us, throwing snow in our faces. Lumley was first, bending into the wind, his fancy topcoat billowing out behind him like a sail. He cast two shadows, one from Tookey's headlights, the other from his own taillights. I was behind him, and Tookey was a step behind me. When I got to the trunk of the Mercedes, Tookey grabbed me.

"Let him go," he said.

"Janey! Francie!" Lumley yelled. "Everything okay?" He pulled open the driver's-side door and leaned in. "Everything—"

He froze to a dead stop. The wind ripped the heavy door right out of his hand and pushed it all the way open.

One for the Road

"Holy God, Booth," Tookey said, just below the scream of the wind. "I think it's happened again."

Lumley turned back toward us. His face was scared and bewildered, his eyes wide. All of a sudden he lunged toward us through the snow, slipping and almost falling. He brushed me away like I was nothing and grabbed Tookey.

"How did you know?" he roared. "Where are they? What the hell is going on here?"

Tookey broke his grip and shoved past him. He and I looked into the Mercedes together. Warm as toast it was, but it wasn't going to be for much longer. The little amber low-fuel light was glowing. The big car was empty. There was a child's Barbie doll on the passenger's floormat. And a child's ski parka was crumpled over the seatback.

Tookey put his hands over his face . . . and then he was gone. Lumley had grabbed him and shoved him right back into the snowbank. His face was pale and wild. His mouth was working as if he had chewed down on some bitter stuff he couldn't yet unpucker enough to spit out. He reached in and grabbed the parka.

"Francie's coat?" he kind of whispered. And then loud, bellowing: "*Francie's coat!*" He turned around, holding it in front of him by the little fur-trimmed hood. He looked at me, blank and unbelieving. "She can't be out without her coat on, Mr. Booth. Why . . . why . . . she'll freeze to death."

"Mr. Lumley—"

He blundered past me, still holding the parka, shouting:

"*Francie! Janey! Where are you? Where are youuu?*"

I gave Tookey my hand and pulled him onto his feet. "Are you all—"

"Never mind me," he says. "We've got to get hold of him, Booth."

We went after him as fast as we could, which wasn't very fast with the snow hip-deep in some places. But then he stopped and we caught up to him.

"Mr. Lumley—" Tookey started, laying a hand on his shoulder.

"This way," Lumley said. "This is the way they went. Look!"

We looked down. We were in a kind of dip here, and most of the wind went right over our heads. And you could see two sets of tracks, one large and one small, just filling up with snow. If we had been five minutes later, they would have been gone.

He started to walk away, his head down, and Tookey grabbed him back. "No! No, Lumley!"

Lumley turned his wild face up to Tookey's and made a fist. He drew it back . . . but something in Tookey's face made him falter. He looked from Tookey to me and then back again.

"She'll freeze," he said, as if we were a couple of stupid kids. "Don't you get it? She doesn't have her jacket on and she's only seven years old—"

"They could be anywhere," Tookey said. "You can't follow those tracks. They'll be gone in the next drift."

"What do you suggest?" Lumley yells, his voice high and hysterical. "If we go back to get the police, she'll freeze to death! Francie *and* my wife!"

"They may be frozen already," Tookey said. His eyes caught Lumley's. "Frozen, or something worse."

"What do you mean?" Lumley whispered. "Get it straight, goddamn it! Tell me!"

"Mr. Lumley," Tookey says, "there's something in the Lot—"

But I was the one who came out with it finally, said the word I never expected to say. "Vampires, Mr. Lumley. Jerusalem's Lot is full of vampires. I expect that's hard for you to swallow—"

He was staring at me as if I'd gone green. "Loonies," he whispers. "You're a couple of loonies." Then he turned away, cupped his hands around his mouth, and bellowed, *"FRANCIE! JANEY!"* He started floundering off again. The snow was up to the hem of his fancy coat.

I looked at Tookey. "What do we do now?"

"Follow him," Tookey says. His hair was plastered with snow, and he *did* look a little bit loony. "I can't just leave him out here, Booth. Can you?"

"No," I says. "Guess not."

So we started to wade through the snow after Lumley as best we could. But he kept getting further and further ahead. He had his youth to spend, you see. He was breaking the trail, going through that snow like a bull. My arthritis began to bother me something terrible, and I started to look down at my legs, telling myself: A little further, just a little further, keep goin', damn it, keep goin' . . .

I piled right into Tookey, who was standing spread-legged in a drift. His head was hanging and both of his hands were pressed to his chest.

"Tookey," I says, "you okay?"

"I'm all right," he said, taking his hands away. "We'll stick with him, Booth, and when he fags out he'll see reason."

We topped a rise and there was Lumley at the bottom, looking desperately for more tracks. Poor man, there wasn't a chance he was going to find them. The wind blew straight across down there where he was, and any tracks would have been rubbed out three minutes after they was made, let alone a couple of hours.

He raised his head and screamed into the night: *"FRAN-CIE! JANEY! FOR GOD'S SAKE!"* And you could hear the desperation in his voice, the terror, and pity him for it. The only answer he got was the freight-train wail of the wind. It almost seemed to be laughin' at him, saying: *I took them Mister New Jersey with your fancy car and cam-el's-hair topcoat. I took them and I rubbed out their tracks and by morning I'll have them just as neat and frozen as two strawberries in a deepfreeze . . .*

"Lumley!" Tookey bawled over the wind. "Listen, you never mind vampires or boogies or nothing like that, but you mind this! You're just making it worse for them! We got to get the—"

And then there *was* an answer, a voice coming out of the dark like little tinkling silver bells, and my heart turned cold as ice in a cistern.

"Jerry . . . Jerry, is that you?"

Lumley wheeled at the sound. And then *she* came, drifting out of the dark shadows of a little copse of trees like a ghost. She was a city woman, all right, and right then she seemed like the most beautiful woman I had ever seen. I felt like I wanted to go to her and tell her how glad I was she was safe after all. She was wearing a heavy green pullover sort of thing, a poncho, I believe they're called. It floated all around her, and her dark hair streamed out in the wild wind like water in a December creek, just before the winter freeze stills it and locks it in.

Maybe I did take a step toward her, because I felt Tookey's hand on my shoulder, rough and warm. And still—how can I say it?—I *yearned* after her, so dark and beautiful with that green poncho floating around her neck and shoulders, so exotic and strange as to make you think of some beautiful woman from a Walter de la Mare poem.

"Janey!" Lumley cried. *"Janey!"* He began to struggle through the snow toward her, his arms outstretched.

"No!" Tookey cried. *"No, Lumley!"*

He never even looked . . . but she did. She looked up at us and grinned. And when she did, I felt my longing, my yearning turn to horror as cold as the grave, as white and silent as bones in a shroud. Even from the rise we could see the sullen red glare in those eyes. They were less human than a wolf's eyes. And when she grinned you could see how long her teeth had become. She wasn't human anymore. She was a dead thing somehow come back to life in this black howling storm.

Tookey made the sign of the cross at her. She flinched back . . . and then grinned at us again. We were too far away, and maybe too scared.

"Stop it!" I whispered. "Can't we stop it?"

"Too late, Booth!" Tookey says grimly.

Lumley had reached her. He looked like a ghost himself, coated in snow like he was. He reached for her . . . and then he began to scream. I'll hear that sound in my dreams, that man screaming like a child in a nightmare. He tried to back away from her, but her arms, long and bare and as white as the snow, snaked out and pulled him to her. I could see her cock her head and then thrust it forward—

"Booth!" Tookey said hoarsely. "We've got to get out of here!"

And so we ran. Ran like rats, I suppose some would say, but those who would weren't there that night. We fled back down along our own backtrail, falling down, getting up again, slipping and sliding. I kept looking back over my shoulder to see if that woman was coming after us, grinning that grin and watching us with those red eyes.

We got back to the Scout and Tookey doubled over, holding his chest. "Tookey!" I said, badly scared. "What—"

"Ticker," he said. "Been bad for five years or more. Get

me around in the shotgun seat, Booth, and then get us the hell out of here."

I hooked an arm under his coat and dragged him around and somehow boosted him up and in. He leaned his head back and shut his eyes. His skin was waxy-looking and yellow.

I went back around the hood of the truck at a trot, and I damned near ran into the little girl. She was just standing there beside the driver's-side door, her hair in pigtails, wearing nothing but a little bit of a yellow dress.

"Mister," she said in a high, clear voice, as sweet as morning mist, "won't you help me find my mother? She's gone and I'm so cold—"

"Honey," I said, "honey, you better get in the truck. Your mother's—"

I broke off, and if there was ever a time in my life I was close to swooning, that was the moment. She was standing there, you see, but she was standing *on top* of the snow and there were no tracks, not in any direction.

She looked up at me then, Lumley's daughter Francie. She was no more than seven years old, and she was going to be seven for an eternity of nights. Her little face was a ghastly corpse white, her eyes a red and silver that you could fall into. And below her jaw I could see two small punctures like pinpricks, their edges horribly mangled.

She held out her arms at me and smiled. "Pick me up, mister," she said softly. "I want to give you a kiss. Then you can take me to my mommy."

I didn't want to, but there was nothing I could do. I was leaning forward, my arms outstretched. I could see her mouth opening, I could see the little fangs inside the pink ring of her lips. Something slipped down her chin, bright and silvery, and with a dim, distant, faraway horror, I realized she was drooling.

Her small hands clasped themselves around my neck and I was thinking: Well, maybe it won't be so bad, not so bad, maybe it won't be so awful after a while—when something black flew out of the Scout and struck her on the chest. There was a puff of strange-smelling smoke, a flashing glow that was gone an instant later, and then she was backing away, hissing. Her face was twisted into a vulpine mask of rage, hate, and pain. She turned sideways and then . . . and then she was gone. One moment she was there and the next there was a twisting knot of snow that looked a little bit like a human shape. Then the wind tattered it away across the fields.

"Booth!" Tookey whispered. "Be quick, now!"

And I was. But not so quick that I didn't have time to pick up what he had thrown at that little girl from hell. His mother's Douay Bible.

That was some time ago. I'm a sight older now, and I was no chicken then. Herb Tooklander passed on two years ago. He went peaceful, in the night. The bar is still there, some man and his wife from Waterville bought it, nice people, and they've kept it pretty much the same. But I don't go by much. It's different somehow with Tookey gone.

Things in the Lot go on pretty much as they always have. The sheriff found that fellow Lumley's car the next day, out of gas, the battery dead. Neither Tookey nor I said anything about it. What would have been the point? And every now and then a hitchhiker or a camper will disappear around there someplace, up on Schoolyard Hill or out near the Harmony Hill cemetery. They'll turn up the fellow's packsack or a paperback book all swollen and bleached out by the rain or snow, or some such. But never the people.

I still have bad dreams about that stormy night we went out there. Not about the woman so much as the little girl, and the way she smiled when she held her arms up so I could pick her up. So she could give me a kiss. But I'm an old man and the time comes soon when dreams are done.

You may have an occasion to be traveling in southern Maine yourself one of these days. Pretty part of the country-side. You may even stop by Tookey's Bar for a drink. Nice place. They kept the name just the same. So have your drink, and then my advice to you is to keep right on moving north. Whatever you do, don't go up that road to Jerusalem's Lot.

Especially not after dark.

There's a little girl somewhere out there. And I think she's still waiting for her good-night kiss.

Angelica

by Jane Yolen

He was a boy with a fever he would never outgrow.

The boy could not sleep. It was hot and he had been sick for so long. All night his head had throbbed. Finally he sat up and managed to get out of bed. He went down the stairs without stumbling.

Elated at his progress, he slipped from the house without waking either his mother or father. His goal was the river bank. He had not been there in a month.

He had always considered the river bank his own. No one else in the family ever went there. He liked to set his feet in the damp ground and make patterns. It was like a picture, and the artist in him appreciated the primitive beauty.

Heat lightning jetted across the sky. He sat down on a fallen log and picked at the bark as he would a scab. He could feel the log imprint itself on his backside through

the thin cotton pajamas. He wished—not for the first time—
that he could be allowed to sleep without his clothes.

The silence and heat enveloped him. He closed his eyes
and dreamed of sleep, but his head still throbbed. He had
never been out at night by himself before. The slight touch
of fear was both pleasure and pain.

He thought about that fear, probing it like a loose tooth,
now to feel the ache and now to feel the sweetness, when
the faint came upon him and he tumbled slowly from the
log. There was nothing but river bank before him, nothing
to slow his descent, and he rolled down the slight hill and
into the river, not waking till the shock of the water hit
him.

It was cold and unpleasantly muddy. He thrashed about.
The sour water got in his mouth and made him gag.

Suddenly someone took his arm and pulled him up onto
the bank, dragged him up the slight incline.

He opened his eyes and shook his head to get the lank,
wet hair from his face. He was surprised to find that his
rescuer was a girl, about his size, in a white cotton shift.
She was not muddied at all from her efforts. His one thought
before she heaved him over the top of the bank and helped
him back onto the log was that she must be quite marvelously
strong.

"Thank you," he said, when he was seated again, and
then did not know where to go from there.

"You are welcome." Her voice was low, her speech precise, almost old-fashioned in its carefulness. He realized that she was not a girl but a small woman.

"You fell in," she said.

"Yes."

She sat down beside him and looked into his eyes, smiling. He wondered how he could see so well when the moon was behind her. She seemed to light up from within like some kind of lamp. Her outline was a golden glow and her blonde hair fell in straight lengths to her shoulder.

"You may call me Angelica," she said.

"Is that your name?"

She laughed. "No. No, it is not. And how perceptive of you to guess."

"Is it an alias?" He knew about such things. His father was a customs official and told the family stories at the table about his work.

"It is the name I . . ." she hesitated for a moment and looked behind her. Then she turned and laughed again. "It is the name I travel under."

"Oh."

"You could not pronounce my real name," she said.

"Could I try?"

"*Pistias Sophia!*" said the woman and she stood as she named herself. She seemed to shimmer and grow at her own words, but the boy thought that might be the fever in his head, though he hadn't a headache anymore.

"Pissta. . . ." he could not stumble around the name.

There seemed to be something blocking his tongue. "I guess I better call you Angelica for now," he said.

"For now," she agreed.

He smiled shyly at her. "My name is Addie," he said.

"I know."

"How do you know? Do I look like an Addie? It means . . ."

"Noble hero," she finished for him.

"How do you know *that?*"

"I am very wise," she said. "And names are important to me. To all . . . of us. Destiny is in names." She smiled, but her smile was not so pleasant any longer. She started to reach for his hand, but he drew back.

"You shouldn't boast," he said. "About being wise. It's not nice."

"I am not boasting." She found his hand and held it in hers. Her touch was cool and infinitely soothing. She reached over with the other hand and put it first palm, then back to his forehead. She made a "tch" against her teeth and scowled. "Your guardian should be Flung Over. I shall have to speak to Uriel about this. Letting you out with such a fever."

"Nobody *let* me out," said the boy. "I let myself out. No one knows I am here—except you."

"Well, there is one who *should* know where you are. And he shall certainly hear from me about this." She stood up and was suddenly much taller than the boy. "Come.

Back to the house with you. You should be in bed." She reached down the front of her white shift and brought up a silver bottle on a chain. "You must take a sip of this now. It will help you sleep."

"Will you come back with me?" the boy asked after taking a drink.

"Just a little way." She held his hand as they went.

He looked behind once to see his footprints in the rain-soft earth. They marched in an orderly line behind him. He could not see hers at all.

"Do you believe, little Addie?" Her voice seemed to come from a long way off, further even than the hills.

"Believe in what?"

"In God. Do you believe that he directs all our movements?"

"I sing in the church choir," he said, hoping it was the proof she wanted.

"That will do for now," she said.

There was a fierceness in her voice that made him turn in the muddy furrow and look at her. She towered above him, all white and gold and glowing. The moon haloed her head, and behind her, close to her shoulders, he saw something like wings, feathery and waving. He was suddenly desperately afraid.

"What are you?" he whispered.

"What do you think I am?" she asked, and her face looked carved in stone, so white her skin and black the features.

"Are you . . . the angel of death?" he asked and then looked down before she answered. He could not bear to watch her talk.

"For you, I am an angel of life," she said. "Did I not save you?"

"What kind of angel are you?" he whispered, falling to his knees before her.

She lifted him up and cradled him in her arms. She sang him a lullaby in a language he did not know. "I told you in the beginning who I am," she murmured to the sleeping boy. "I am Pistias Sophia, angel of wisdom and faith. The one who put the serpent into the garden, little Adolf. But I was only following orders."

Her wings unfurled behind her. She pumped them once, twice, and then the great wind they commanded lifted her into the air. She flew without a sound to the Hitler house and left the boy sleeping, feverless, in his bed.